Molly

never dreamed of going to the

New Year's Eve bash with her

Postman ...

A novella by

Jan Dargatz

Publisher: Pengold Garrett & Associates, P.O. Box 702870, Tulsa, OK 74170.

Book cover design by David Marshall
Interior design and production by Starr Clay

(dmcreativedirector@me.com)

Printed in the United States of America.

First Edition: August 2011

ISBN: 978-1-937566-17-3

Table of Contents

1

Molly never dreamed of going to the New Year's Eve bash with her postman. Indeed, it would not have made the top one thousand notions on her most random day.

For at least six months, Molly had soundly counted on going to the New Year's Eve extravaganza at the oldest and most prestigious country club in her city with the recently available and supremely desirable bachelor Ian Glossman.

She and Ian had dated exclusively for seven months after his disentanglement from a romantic relationship with a former beauty queen he had known for years. By the time Thanksgiving Day rolled around, Molly and Ian had become enough of a couple for her to be invited to Ian's grandmother's most-definitely-a-mansion for lunch. Mind you, forty-four other people had also been invited to the event, which meant tables in several rooms, and a couple of makeshift wine bars scattered in various lobbies and hallways. Molly and Ian had found a cozy table for eight out in the sunroom and had laughed their way through three thousand calories, including two servings of pie, with six people they had never seen before and were not likely to ever see again. It was a good time, they had both concluded—light, breezy, tasty, and without football.

On the way home, Ian had asked if she wanted to go to the country club ball on New Year's Eve.

Of course! She had counted on it, but acted surprised nonetheless. Ian seemed pleased that she was surprised and didn't appear to have counted on it. Then he had handed her two tickets and said casually, "Hang on to these. I'll probably lose them." She had put them in her favorite wood-inlay box that was just the right size for holding tickets.

Molly wasn't exactly hoping for an engagement ring or proposal by the end of the year, but it was an outside long-shot. Ian had mentioned a number of times the possibility of their making things "official" . . . they had lingered more than once before jewelry stores while window shopping . . . and he had definitely been consulting her about furniture and the interior design of the high-rise loft he was planning to buy and remodel in mid-January. What else was a girl to think? A future with Ian was a lovely idea and there's no better time than the holidays to be in love and think lovely thoughts.

Molly bought the slinkiest black dress she could find on December 2—a perfect fit if she didn't gain an ounce between the time of the purchase and the time of the ball.

The stilettos to go with the dress were a major investment on December 4. That still gave her time to break them in and try a little dancing around the kitchen.

The silk cape as a wrap to wear over her dress was discovered and secured December 6.

By December 7, a hair appointment, harder to come by than she had anticipated, was secured for December 30. Ditto for waxing, manicure, pedicure, and facial. It would be a whole day at the best salon spa in town, her Christmas gift to herself.

The perfect hair bauble was spotted and secured on December 9.

The perfect holiday present for Ian was spotted and secured December 11.

And from then on, her life had been a round of baking the most perfect cookies, wrapping the prettiest presents, and decorating in the tastiest style—effort not lost since Ian had asked her to go shopping with him on three occasions, had solicited her help in wrapping presents on two evenings, had treated her to dinner out twice and had come over for an evening of dinner by her fireplace and an old-fashioned holiday movie four days before Christmas.

On December 23, Ian showed up at her doorstep with an armload of garland, and after helping her hang it over her doorway and up the stairwell, he had turned to her and said without preamble, "Molly, I can't."

"Can't what?" It was an innocent enough question.

"Can't go on."

"Go on where?"

"With you."

Molly sat down on the bottom step of the stairwell and motioned for him to do the same. He remained standing.

"What are you saying?" Molly asked. In her heart she hoped he was leading up to saying something like, "I can't go on without marrying you, so . . . ."

"I haven't been honest. I've been seeing Sterilyn for the past three weeks. She came back to town and called and we've sorta picked up where we left off, and . . . ."

Molly really didn't remember clearly if there was anything said after that. She knew there had been tears that seemed to fly out of her eyes without her permission. Ian had stumbled around hunting for a handkerchief in his back pocket, which he had handed her without touching her, took two steps back, and finally shrugged as if to say without using words, "I'm sorry—such is life," turned, and walked out, pulling the door tightly behind him.

It happened so fast and so definitively, Molly lived in a daze for the next three days. She went to church as planned for the midnight service on Christmas Eve. The carols sounded hollow and the candlelight seemed blurred through tears that puddled but did not flow. She was grateful she didn't see anyone she knew. She didn't stay for the recessional and was home by half past midnight.

She managed to sit through Christmas lunch at her sister's house without anybody asking questions she couldn't answer. It helped that her six-year-old nephew and four-year-old niece were hanging on her arms from the minute she walked in until the minute she walked out.

When on earth did he find time to see Sterilyn when he seemed to be on her doorstep every other minute?

What is this magic hold that Sterilyn has over him?

What a jerk!

What if he is emotionally ill and doesn't know it—would an intervention help?

Why didn't I have any hints that this was on the horizon?

What kind of name is Sterilyn anyway?

At least a dozen other questions entered her mind at odd hours of the day and night, none of which had answers.

The day after Christmas she boxed up everything that spoke of joy and holiday cheer, and when the mailman rang her bell on December 27 to deliver a package too big for the box outside her front door, she took one look at his bright clean-shaven and apparently honest face and said, "Would you like to go to a New Year's Eve party with me?"

Without skipping a beat, he handed her the package and the rest of her mail and said, "Sure."

"Really?" Molly had asked, brushing her hair back to take a closer look at her would-be date.

"Sure."

Molly laughed, awkwardly.

"Well, I'm sure about saying yes if you're sure about the invitation," her mailman said.

"Sure," said Molly. And then she added very directly, "It's a formal ball at the country club." She was almost certain that would bring an end to all this sure-ness.

"Okay. What time should I pick you up?"

"Uh, um, uh . . . nine-thirty."

"Great."

And with that, he smiled—had she ever seen him smile before? Probably. She couldn't recall. It was a very nice smile.

He turned and walked down the walk and toward the next house.

"Thanks!" Molly called after him. That seemed like it *might* be the right thing to say. He turned and waved.

Molly turned and walked into her house, closed the door, and slide down it until she reached the floor.

"What have I done?" she said to Houndcat, who had come into the room to survey this most unusual sight of Molly clutching her knees as she sat with her back against the front door.

Houndcat sniffed at the garland bit that had fallen from the stairwell and didn't reply.

"What have I done!"

2

Molly had never regarded herself as a desperate woman and she refused to adopt that perception two days before New Year's Eve. She rationally and objectively decided that her mailman would ring her doorbell the next day and politely say, "Oh, by the way, I know you were just teasing when you invited me to a New Year's Eve party at a country club. No harm, no foul."

That isn't what happened. Oh, he rang her doorbell the next day right on schedule, but instead of the words she was expecting to hear, he said, "Oh, by the way, my name is Peter Lorgham. I thought you should at least know my name before New Year's."

He said it with the nicest of smiles.

Molly was flustered, "My name is . . . ."

Then she caught herself as he said, "Molly Herman. I know. I deliver your mail."

Of course. Molly smiled and tried to rebound into the conversation, "Clever man to figure that out!"

He smiled back, turned, and was gone.

It was not at all—no, not at all—what she had counted on. It was starting to appear that she just might be going—actually *going*—to the country-club extravaganza after all. And with her *mailman.*

Molly wasn't a snob. She had great respect for all law-abiding, money-earning, tax-paying, respectful-of-others, kind-to-strangers people of all races and nationalities. If pressed on the point, she would have admitted that she had only two black

friends—actually, one of them was only half-black—
no Hispanic friends, and two sorta-friends who were
of Asian descent—they probably fell more into the
category of acquaintances since they were people
with whom she worked but did not socialize. She
probably would have quipped that she liked cheese
grits, chili rellenos, and lo mein with equal passion.

While not owning any form of the "snob"
label, Molly was a person who considered herself a
woman with high standards. She had worked hard
to live in her nice house on a nice street in a nice
neighborhood on a nice side of town. She admired
others who also worked hard and lived a quality
lifestyle. Although she had no grand aspirations to
be exceedingly wealthy, she also had no desire to be
poor. She had worked on Habitat for Humanity
projects, had volunteered on short-term mission
trips to hurricane-ravaged areas, and routinely had
given her castaway clothing to projects that helped
women seeking to move from full-time welfare to
full-time employment. She liked the idea of
sacrificing to help the unfortunate, as long as the
definition of "sacrifice" was left to her, and more
specifically, as long as there was a hot shower and
comfortable bed at the end of any day devoted to
community service.

In her heart of hearts, Molly believed that
most people could do a lot more to improve their
personal economic and social standing in life, and
that they should choose to do so. She had been
known to say, "It doesn't cost anything to go to the
library, go to church, or go to community service
meetings. Get an education, get God, get a reason
for living, and get busy."

It was a simple philosophy, really.

Molly didn't see herself or life in general as being very complicated. "Work hard. Pay taxes. Love whole-heartedly. Sleep well at night."

All of which is to say that a government employee of the postal service variety was not someone she had ever thought about knowing very well, much less cultivating as a friend, much less dating. The idea of a postman's "job" left her feeling a little ambivalent—her mailman obviously worked and was diligent and dependable at working and that was admirable. She quickly scanned her memory bank and concluded that she had never found him negligent in the delivery of her mail, and true to the postal motto, he HAD delivered her mail in rain and sun, sleet, hail, snow, and ice—which was no small feat in that tiny little white postal vehicle. There was something to be said for dedication and dependability.

At the same time, his job was rather predictable and routine and without quick upward advancement, and that made her suspicious about his degree of ambition. She could not fathom that he might have anything of a "world view" or travel experience. She wondered if he had gone to college or ever had any other career, and concluded, *Not likely.*

For two days, Molly found herself returning again and again to a new and fairly long list of questions, which also had no answers:

Why on earth did I spontaneously invite this almost-stranger to a very important party?

Am I a desperate woman who can't bear the thought of being alone on a major social holiday?

Will Ian be at the country club ball with Sterilyn?

What will I say if I encounter him?

Should I call to offer Ian back the tickets in my ticket box?

If I did give the tickets back, what would I say to my postman?

Exactly who is this postman named Peter?

Why did he accept my zany invitation?

Will Peter Lorgham the Postman know how to dance at a ball, or which fork to use at the dinner table?

What on earth will we find to talk about?

Who needs to talk at a ball?

What if he asks me out for a second date?

Why should I be concerned about all these things?

Why not just go to the party and have a great time and laugh a lot later?

She had no answers, except to the question about the tickets. She decided they were hers— consolation prize, gift, secret weapon, whatever. She would go to the party and get better acquainted with her postman, and dance her finest dance in the beautiful stilettos that were now dance-tested and ready for show-time.

In the meantime, she was determined to enjoy her day at the salon spa.

3

"Do you have any wonderful plans for tomorrow night?" the manicurist asked.

It was not Molly's manicurist asking, however. It was the manicurist at the table next to Molly. The woman being asked was pert and pretty, short dark hair and Gucci. "Of course!" she answered happily. "I'm going to the dance at the country club, fine dining and fine wine included."

Molly's attention was captivated in a heartbeat's time. Her own manicurist had been called away to a phone call at the front desk and Molly had been preoccupying herself with looking at various outlandish colors of nail polish on the silver tray set before her. Her reaction would normally have been a smirk to "Silver Lights Up the Night" and "New Year's Dancerama" as colors for nail polish, but today, strange things seemed normal and the colors didn't seem at all bizarre. "Dancerama" had a somewhat colorful sheen to its no-color "clear" . . . almost holographic.

"I've heard the country club ball is so crowded you can hardly dance," the next-door manicurist said.

"Sometimes. The closer it gets to midnight, the more crowded it gets. If you go early, you can get a dance in between food courses," said Gucci girl. "And it's always fun to see who's there even if you are sitting on the sidelines watching."

"Are there sidelines to sit on?" the manicurist asked.

"Sure thing. Dishing about the various couples is a favorite sideline sport."

I'll bet, thought Molly. At which point her own manicurist showed up and together, they decided on "Dance All Night" as the color of the hour. It was a rather vibrant coral with plenty of glitter mixed in. The matching lipstick purchase and extra bottle of polish for touch-ups was extra, of course, but Molly was feeling personally indulgent. *Purchasing a total spa day for yourself should have SOME take-home prize,* she thought wryly.

The manicure and pedicure gave way to a massage and facial in a darkened room filled with gentle music, and Molly was able to dwell on the concept of "sidelines." She concluded that "watching from the sidelines" just might be her ticket out of too much dancing and dining at the ball, and perhaps make her presence and her date less conspicuous.

I wonder where those sidelines are, Molly mentally mused. She envisioned a balcony overlooking the dance floor. She had been to the country club on a number of occasions through the years but not since the latest multi-million-dollar renovation. Surely a balcony *might* have been added?

Of one thing she felt certain. She had no doubt that her mailman would go along with the idea of watching from the sidelines. After all, how conspicuous would *he* want to be in a social setting that was totally alien to him, and therefore, uncomfortable.

Molly couldn't have been more wrong.

4

There are some occasions in which all of one's "getting ready" is filled with minor catastrophes—the chip of a nail, a run in the hosiery, a portion of a hairdo that just will not cooperate. This was not one of those times. Everything slid on, slicked down, and zipped up without incident.

Molly found herself with just enough time to get nervous before the doorbell rang. And then, there he was. Peter Lorgham on her doorstep wearing a perfectly fitting tuxedo and holding a long-stemmed yellow rose.

Handing her the rose he said, "They tell me that a yellow rose is a sign of friendship. I hope that's the case—not only for the flower, but the night."

Molly smiled and, holding the rose to her nose, she said, "It even has aroma. Most roses don't, you know."

"Yeah," he replied. "They lose it someplace over Ecuador, I think."

"Ecuador?"

"On their way from being grown and cut in Chile."

"Of course."

Hmmm. He might have a world-view, Molly thought. *This is a bit unsettling.*

Houndcat sniffed around Peter Lorgham's ankles and Molly quickly shooed the cat away with a "Scat, Houndcat." Then turning to Peter she said, "This old cat doesn't see many tuxedos."

"Aha," Peter replied with a shrug and yet another award-winning smile. "I was glad it still fit. I bought it three years ago, I think, and am just hoping any aroma of mothballs is overpowered by the aroma of yellow rose."

"I had thought I might put this in a vase, but since you said what you just did, I think I might carry it with me!" Molly said with a spontaneous laugh.

He OWNS this tuxedo? Molly thought. *He just might not be your average postman.*

For his part, Peter Lorgham was thinking, *She'll be the only woman in a red-and-green room with a yellow rose, but that's just fine with me. She'll stand out and that's worthy of her.*

Stepping out into the clear cold night, Molly was surprised to find a limo in her driveway. Not a stretch. More like a limo a wealthy person might own for personal everyday use. Complete with a driver on payroll. *I wonder how he arranged this?* she thought but didn't ask.

They commented on the lighting displays at several houses on the way to the country club. "It's a little strange, don't you think," Peter said, "that we here in America decorate our rooftops and eves in such lavish style? Fake icicles and all. I don't know another country on earth that decorates its houses, except perhaps for the odd palace or two."

"Yes," Molly added, "and then we only wrap lights around the trunks of trees, so they look a bit like pillars with unruly anonymous black-tangled top-knots."

"And what's with the oversized balloon figures of Santa and Frosty? How do you suppose they blow up those things, and keep them inflated?"

"And what about the new trend to have lighting patterns synchronized to sound tracks?"

Peter Lorgham was an easy conversationalist who apparently knew more than the local ZIP codes. Molly was starting to think that the evening might be a pleasant one after all.

"Good evening, Mr. Lorgham," the country-club valet parking attendant said as he opened the door of the limo. "I'm assuming that you will want Max to park for you."

"Yes, thank you Carlos," said Peter. Max, for his part, had opened the door to allow Molly to leave the limo.

The doorman knows Peter Lorgham?
He knows THEIR names?
What's happening?

Molly hoped her face didn't give evidence of her surprise that was on the borderline of shock.

The coat-check girl and a waiter carrying a large silver tray of champagne flutes also seemed to know her date by name. *Is this some type of dream?*

"You seem to know this place," Molly commented. "And they know you . . . ."

Peter Lorgham smiled and shrugged and casually semi-nodded a yes.

They moved easily into the main hall where the hostess said simply, "Good evening, Mr. Lorgham. I'll show you to your table."

The tickets to the ball were still buried in Molly's handbag. "I didn't know my tickets to this ball included a 'table,'" she said.

"They don't," said Peter. "The ball is up the staircase. The tables are for hot hors d'oeuvres with waiter service. I thought it might be a good way to begin, especially since the upstairs ballroom doesn't have a very good view of the new swimming hole, and no food."

Sure enough . . . the pool was resplendent with giant floating poinsettias that seemed aglow with candles, a theme that spilled over into the glassed-in dining area with its floor-to-ceiling windows and electric chimineas decked in holiday array. Greenery and white twinkle lights, oversized silk poinsettias in a full range of red, white, pink, and variegated varieties, oversized gold ribbon in three designs, and dozens upon dozens of fake candles adding a softening touch of "glow" to the room . . . crystal chandeliers decked with greenery and still more poinsettias tablecloths of red velvet with crystal candleholders and red candles; and crystal chargers big enough to hold poinsettia designed plates, champagne flute; and a poinsettia napkin with a silver fork . . . it was all slightly beyond fantasia.

"It's beautiful," said Molly softly as they were seated at a table for two in a corner close to the window overlooking the pool.

"A bit over the top," Peter noted. "But I'm a sucker for holiday glitz. If you're going to have glitz, you ought to have just slightly too much of it, in my opinion." He liked the look of awe on Molly's face. *Childlike innocence,* he thought, *even if she isn't a child and may not be all that innocent. . . . Or then again, she might be.* It was a thought he found worthy of entertaining.

Molly noted his slight sense of distraction and the subtle smile, and raised her eyebrows in a silent question.

"Just musing a bit," said Peter. "So much glitz makes my mind wander."

"I'm not sure this is all real," Molly said with an air of resignation to the notion that she just might be asleep and in the midst of a phenomenal dream.

"I don't think any of it is real," Peter said. "Just the illusion of evergreens and poinsettias."

"I mean the overall night so far," Molly said. "Not quite real."

"Oh," Peter replied.

"I wasn't expecting all this," she said, feeling a need to explain herself—her eyes taking in the room as whole. "I wasn't expecting you in a tux or to show up in a limo or for everybody here to know your name."

"Oh," he said again.

"Are you real?" she asked, leaning across the table just slightly and looking at him as if examining a curio.

"More real than anything else in this room except you," he said quietly and intensely. *This is most definitely NOT what I ever envisioned*, Molly concluded. *Who IS this mailman of mine?*

And at that, a waiter came to the table. Without asking Molly for any suggestions and without consulting any menu, Peter Lorgham proceeded to order a small plate of appetizers for her, as if he already knew the full selection available. The waiter scribbled quickly as Peter concluded, "412." The waiter nodded, said, "Thank you, Mr. Lorgham," and backed away.

Before Molly could say anything further— more than a little curious as to how it was that her postman was obviously a member of the oldest and finest country club in a three-state region—she heard a vaguely familiar voice from over her left shoulder, "Peter! Peter! Darling Peter! I'm so glad you came this evening."

She turned to see Ian Glossman's grandmother.

"Grams," Peter said, rising to give the woman a gentle hug.

Molly gripped both sides of the table firmly. She was certain that if she let go, she'd fall to the floor in a dead faint.

5

With his hands remaining on her upper arms after a generous hug, Peter appraised the appearance of the woman before him and concluded, "Hands down, the most stunning woman in the room over the age of forty."

"And what about under forty?" Grams replied with spunk.

"Can't diminish the appearance of my date," Peter laughed, and so did Grams, who turned to study Molly for the first time.

"Molly Herman," Peter said in a mock announcer's voice, pointing to her as if to the prizes on a game show. And then turning to the older woman, "My grandmother, Mirabelle Glossman."

Molly started to rise, her hand outstretched. "Oh do stay seated, dear," Mrs. Glossman said. "I'm pleased to meet you." And then with a question mark of possible recognition crossing her face, she added, "Or should I say, I'm pleased to see you *again*. I'm wondering if we have met in the past?"

"Yes," said Molly. "I was in your home for Thanksgiving Dinner."

"Oh, yes!" said Mrs. Glossman. "You are the young woman who wrote the most beautiful thank-you note on that very elegant stationery—in fact, you wrote one of only four thank-you notes I received. Very appreciated, my dear, very appreciated."

Then, turning to Peter she added, "This one of my grandsons is far less of a cad."

Before Peter could say anything she flashed a smile that lit up the entire room and turned with a flair to walk jauntily to a table nearby.

Molly regripped the edges of the table. The room was spinning, she was sure of it.

"I think when her parents named her Mirabelle they had an inkling that she'd be the belle of any ball she attended. She's always had that sauciness about her."

"Over a serious layer of deeply embedded elegance," Molly added.

"Indeed, oh yes, indeed. Nobody does elegance like Grams. But she also has a sense of theater about her. My cousin used to call her Mirrorball—of the disco variety, you know. She can have a blinding, dizzying quality to her that seems to fragment the immediate environment and almost makes you forget your name—and at the same time, makes you want to dance with abandon."

"Your cousin?"

"Ian Glassman," said Peter matter-of-factly, not at all unnerved by her lack of segue from one topic to the next. "He *was* your escort for Grams' T-day bash, wasn't he?"

Molly nodded. It seemed so long ago. *And how did he know?*

"Distant memory," she said.

"Or quick recovery," Peter said without skipping a beat. She wasn't at all sure whether he was referring to her skillful repartee, or to the mending of her smashed-up heart. And frankly, in that moment, she wasn't sure either.

6

The next two hours passed in a blur or color, light, and borderline euphoria. The hot hors'doeuvres—a nice blend of bite-sized meats, seafood, cheese, and vegetable concoctions—were followed by an equally nice blend of bite-sized sweets, both cake-based and fruit. All were devoured with at least a dozen "mmm's" of appreciation—both for their presentation and taste. The champagne seemed ever-flowing, but Molly was smart enough to keep her wits about her and rarely took a sip. She noticed that Peter did the same.

Somehow the night had become too important to mess up, which was what over-indulgence usually created. They talked and laughed easily about various people in the room, childhood experiences with Christmas, the food, and the mood.

About 10:45 or so they wandered up the gently winding staircase to the official country club ballroom, which was decked out in only slightly less glitter and glam than the dining room below. No jazz combo here—rather, a full old-fashioned big-band dance-band. Peter admitted to having once played the tenor sax in such a band. Molly admitted to having listened to all of her grandfather's 78-rpm recordings of the Glen Miller band and clarinetist Benny Goodman. They agreed on their partiality for "String of Pearls," "Take the A Train," and "Chattanooga Choo-Choo." And they also agreed that slow dances were better than fast ones in a crowded venue, and especially under the glitz of a disco mirror ball.

"Disco and big band somehow working together, and way too many dancers" was Peter's two-part appraisal of the room.

"Glad for the no-back benches at the edges of the room, and a great band leader with a sense of humor" was Molly's take.

They laughed some more when the music was too loud, communicated with raised eyebrows, a roll of the eyes, and thumbs up or down signals.

Upon entering the ballroom and for the first forty minutes there, Molly found herself gazing about the room. She told herself that it was interesting to see who was there and what people were wearing. In truth, of course, she was scanning the crowd for a sign of Ian Glossman, whom she fully expected to see draped around Sterilyn. She was hoping that if, indeed, that was the case, Sterilyn would be wearing a dress identical to three other women in the room, although she also admitted that was unlikely. For her part, Molly was grateful that in her scanning of both the dining room and ballroom she had not seen her own dress on any other woman. The extra dollars had been worth exclusivity after all.

After forty minutes, Molly stopped caring who was there, who was with whom, or what people were wearing. She found herself fully focused on the man in front of her and the beat of the band.

Peter Lorgham turned out to be a great dancer in Molly's opinion—he was the kind of man who could lead a woman into being a better dancer than she really was or had ever been, even in stilettos. He was especially good at innovating moves in a radius of five feet, which is about all any couple had on the increasingly crowded dance floor.

Eventually that radius became closer to forty inches, which meant all moves were slow-dance moves.

Molly was not sorry about that. There was a nice fit in dancing slow dances with Peter Lorgham—he was just taller-enough, and held her just tight enough.

She was increasingly aware that the clock was ticking ever closer to midnight—11:48 to be exact on the extremely oversized clock hung midst garland and ribbon above the big band at the front of the ballroom.

Why haven't I thought about midnight before now?

Will my dance partner kiss me?

Surely he will, it would be too awkward NOT to—

but will he attempt a kiss on the lips?

Will he be passionate or cordial?

Will he apologize afterward?

Will such a kiss—either way—change anything?

She pondered whether she should excuse herself and head for the ladies room, but decided that was a coward's way out. And besides, she was on the verge of WANTING this kiss to be spectacular.

And it was.

Peter gently took her face in both of his hands and after a whispered, "Happy New Year, Molly" he delivered a kiss that was straight out of the movies—long, gentle, passionate, and longer-still. When Molly was just on the verge of buckled knees, and just as the singing of "Auld Lang Syne" ended, he released her face only to put his arms around her in a huge bear hug, lifting her and twirling her a full circle with her feet several inches off the ground.

"Happy New Year, Peter," she whispered in his ear.

Wow. She sure hoped it would be happy— the new year, that is. Confetti and dropping balloons and cheers and all.

7

They stayed to dance a bring-on-the-year jitterbug and then made their way toward the exit with a brief stop by the coat-check stand. When offered tall glass mugs of hot chocolate with whipped cream and peppermint sticks by a waiter carrying a full silver tray of the drinks into the foyer, they decided to avail themselves of one final Christmas sweet. Peter phoned for his driver and then announced to Molly that his driver had just described the crush of people outside the country-club entrance "massive."

"We might as well warm up on the inside before we brave the cold outside," he said.

Molly nodded agreement. As they sat on a settee in the lobby she asked, "What does 'Auld Lang Syne' mean, anyway?"

"I've heard it means 'Once upon a time,'" said Peter.

"Appropriate," she said. And then thought to herself . . . *I wonder how Robert Burns might have said 'and they lived happily ever after'?*

They didn't talk further. There was no need to, really. Max had put Christmas music on the CD player. The drive home was slow and steady— twenty minutes just to leave the country club grounds—all in all, it was just time for Molly to thoroughly relax in the cradle of Peter's arm.

"Penny for your thoughts," Peter said as they neared her neighborhood. "You haven't said more than four words since midnight."

She replied softly, "They say a kiss isn't over until the person kissed changes the subject."

He turned her face toward him. "So why are you talking now?"

He kissed her again, equally sweet and lingering, but nothing that spoke of insistence that the evening continue after their arrival at her home.

"This has been an amazing night," said Molly.

Peter said, "Just think—we've known each other for two years now," quickly adding for clarification, "Before midnight and after."

Molly grimaced.

"Did I say something with which you disagree, Miss Herman?"

"No," said Molly. "I took off my shoes and I just tried to put one of them back on. I'm not sure it's going to cooperate. I may need to run barefoot from the car to my front door."

"I have a better idea," said Peter. "Don't move. Hand me your front door key and hang on to your shoes."

When they arrived in her drive, Peter got out of the car and trotted to her front door, unlocked it, and partially opened it. He then returned to the car, opened her door, helped her out and scooped her up in his arms in one swift movement, and within seconds, deposited her in her own entryway.

Houndcat was there with a surprised "meouw" and a flourish of his long tail.

After saying a quick goodnight and locking the door, Molly turned to her beloved cat, "I know, I know. It isn't at all what I thought would be happening ten days ago."

8

Molly had half-hoped that Peter would call her the next morning and perhaps might even come over to enjoy French Toast and the Rose Parade with her. As it turned out, she enjoyed a quiet breakfast on her own and was midway through the parade when Tams called.

"So, time to catch up!" said her best friend since first grade. "Dish, dish. What did the handsome Ian Glossman give you for Christmas and is there a wedding date yet?"

It all seemed like terribly old news.

"Oh, dear," said Molly. "You are so last year, Tams!"

"What's that supposed to mean?"

"In a nutshell, Ian dropped me and my mailman picked me up."

The two seconds of stunned silence spoke volumes.

"Whole story, details and more details," said Tams, something of an acronym for Tabitha Pamela Short, whom many in the first grade had called Pammy and the teacher called Tabitha. Molly had come up with Tams and it stuck—not just for their relationship but almost universally. Best friends can have that sort of influence, after all.

An hour and a half later Molly had exhausted all she knew, and she, in turn, had heard about Tam's after-Christmas trip to Jamaica with her two daughters, her two sisters, and her two nieces. "Lance had to work," explained Tams, "but it was okay. I had a great time—girl party to the max."

Tams gave her a full run-down on each one of her six traveling companions. "And I take it the brothers-in-law also had to work?" Molly asked.

"Yep," said Tammy. "End of the year inventory for both of them. But speaking of taking stock of things . . . ."

"I've been doing some of that!" said Molly.

"You don't sound all that sad about the Ian thing," Tams had said during their conversation, and Molly realized that her immediate grief had vanished amazingly fast. "And you do sound excited about this Peter person," Tam's had added. And again, Molly admitted that he was intriguing on many fronts. She was also vaguely disconcerted that she had so few answers about Peter Lorgham. "You need to do some investigative reporting," Tams advised, and added, "Then call me back!"

The questions were certainly many. The answers few. But how to pursue the questions without *sounding* like an investigative reporter? Google provided virtually no clues, and no, he wasn't on Facebook.

Peter called at 12:45. "I gave you plenty of time for beauty sleep and then you were on the phone throughout the parade, so here I am—a federal holiday in my favor, no mail to schlep, and eager to take you out for barbecue later today. Unless, of course you have other plans."

"How did you know I was watching the parade?"

"I didn't. But I was watching it. Had to see who won the Governor's Trophy, you know."

Molly laughed. "The same people who won it the last three years, or so the announcer said."

"So you *were* watching the parade!"

"Yes, and barbecue later today sounds great."

"I'll pick you up about four?" Peter suggested.

"I'll be ready."

Molly was pleased. There was no awkwardness, and not one bit of apology or questioning on Peter's part as to whether it was "too much" to be calling "too soon" after their first and only date. She had absolutely no desire to play hard to get.

Peter showed up at four minutes to four o'clock in a silver gray two-seater Lexus. "My other car is a beat-up ol' red Ford pickup," he said wryly. "Just so you'll know."

"I thought it was a limo," Molly replied with a little laugh.

"Oh, that's my OTHER other car," said Peter. "Every guy should have three vehicles, don't you think? One for the big and important occasions, one for going very fast—or at least looking as if you *could* go very fast, and one for doing the basic down-and-dirty chores of life."

"By all means," said Molly. "I, on the other hand, have figured out how to have just one car for all three purposes."

"You're a girl," said Peter. "Guys are different."

Yes, thought Molly, *and three cars are a LOT for any person, and especially for a postman.*

They headed for Big Jim's and ordered a platter of ribs and smoked bologna accompanied by heaps of potato salad and baked beans, further accompanied by a trip to Big Jim's famous pickle bar with its six varieties of dilled, sweet, and otherwise-spiced cucumbers and peppers. It was a feast worth savoring slowly, and so they did. Ninety minutes of slow eating and sipping sweet iced tea.

They both agreed that they had eaten to the point just beyond full, and were using the handiwipes provided by the waiter when Molly said, "Nobody does BBQ quite like Big Jim's."

"I agree," said Peter. "It's almost as good—maybe *as* good—as Miller's Smoke House."

Miller's Smoke House?
What would he know about Miller's Smoke House?

"Isn't that the name of the place just a mile or so off I-40 down by Langstrom?" asked Peter, noting her momentary puzzlement.

"Yes," said Molly simply. "What do you know about Miller's Smoke House?"

"Part deli, part café, part truckstop, great hickory smoke lingering in the air, the best Texas toast I've ever eaten."

"You've been there," said Molly matter-of-factly. Her stomach was suddenly churning but she refused to let it show in her voice or on her face. *Peter Lorgham of limo and country club favor had been to HER Miller's Smoke House?*

"Many times," replied Peter. "You seem surprised."

"I am," said Molly. "It almost sounds as if you are surprised that I'm surprised—that you know I'd know about Miller's."

Peter was silent, giving away only a slight smile.

"I didn't really expect you to remember."

"Give me a clue," Molly said. "Remember what exactly?"

"Great granddad Insmore—I called him Boppa—had a spread down that way. My brother Derrick and I spent several summers there, learning to do all sorts of things that are no doubt highly useful for a rural life, and somewhat useful for a city life if you think in terms of discipline and logic and reading the signs of nature . . . .

"Things like roping calves and branding them, feeding chickens and gathering their eggs, learning to chop firewood and stoking a cast-iron stove with just the right amount of wood to take the chill off a cool late-spring, early-summer night . . . .

"And things like learning to bait a hook and catch a catfish in a big pond owned by a family named Herman."

Molly was stunned.

That was her pond he was taking about. The Insmores had the spread next to theirs. Miller's had been the only restaurant she had known before the age of ten. *Had she known Peter as a child? It was sounding that way.*

"So, we knew each other twenty-five years ago?" she asked.

"A little," said Peter.

"You had pigtails and freckles. Could climb a tree better than Derrick and almost as good as me. Could catch a fish faster than both of us. Had a tag-along pal named Tammy, or Tam, or something like that?

"Tams."

"Right. Short for something, right?"

"Tabitha Pamela Short. I gave her the name Tams so she could escape being Tabby or Pammy."

31

"You were a good friend!" Peter responded.

Peter continued, "Ian was there one summer with us. You couldn't quite get his name right—kept calling him Lyman, so Derrick and I played along and even though Ian didn't like it, he became Lyman for years at our various family gatherings. You renamed more than one person!"

The memories were starting to come into focus. She remembered the rather awkward city-slicker boy named Lyman—totally unskilled at anything befitting a ranch boy. Wore funny clothes—her first introduction to khakis and button-downs. Hair always slicked just so. A year or so older. *Lyman was Ian Glossman?* Her head was spinning.

"Did I call you Peter?" she asked.

"You called me Petie-Eye," he said. "At first I thought it was P . . . D . . . I . . . and I couldn't figure out what it stood for. Then I figured that Petie was short for Peter and the 'eye' was for the first letter of my grandfather's last name—Insmore. I knew you were teasing when you called me Petie-Eye, but frankly, I didn't mind. You were a cute little thing and I knew you were just trying to get my attention."

"Aha," said Molly. "Not quite sure I agree totally with that appraisal, but . . . ."

"I don't like to think you were putting me down," said Peter, "although that is also a possibility."

"We didn't really play together, though," said Molly, the images of her past starting to gel a bit. "You were a lot older. A big kid. Your brother was more my age."

"Right," confirmed Peter. "I was twelve or thirteen the first summer. You were maybe seven or eight. We saw each other the most for the first two years I was down on the ranch. The other years, Boppa had serious work for me to do. Considered me on the payroll and treated me like the other hired hands—which was good, just not overly favoring. Took me hunting. Taught me to track deer and rabbits. Not a lot of free time. Derrick saw you more than I did. You called him Outsmore. Not quite sure why."

"He was terrible at softball, as I recall," said Molly. "Both Tams and I could get him to strike out more times than he ever came close to hitting a ball and getting to first base."

"Finally makes sense. Insmore. Outsmore. You've got this thing about names, don't you?"

"I call it a hobby."

"I remember watching a couple of those softball games," said Peter. "I didn't let you drag me into them because I knew as a much older man, I would be expected to play well—and frankly, baseball was never my best game. I was much better at basketball, and just so you'll know and perhaps think better of him, Derrick turned out to be a pretty good football player. Lettered in high school. Played a bit in college even."

"So you've known for awhile that I was little Molly Herman and you never said anything?" asked Molly.

Peter was slow in replying. "I wasn't stalking you, if that's what you are thinking," he said. "And I wasn't playing a strange version of hide and seek."

"What were you playing?" Molly asked. "Is *playing* the right word to use?"

"No," said Peter indignantly. "It is *not* the right word. No games. I delivered mail to M.

Herman for almost two months before I caught a glimpse of you one day planting bulbs in your front flowerbed. You were wearing a red and white striped T-shirt like one I remember you wearing as a kid. And you had your hair pulled back into a loose single braid. It was a flashback moment. I said 'Molly' almost instinctively, not realizing you were close enough to hear me. You looked up from your planting and said, 'Yes?' And I said, 'Here's your mail.'"

"Was that just this last fall?" Molly asked.

"No, a year before."

"And all this time you never said, 'Hey, I think we knew each other as kids?'"

Peter shrugged.

"Technically," he said slowly, "I work for you. You are one of those taxpayers who pays the salaries of those of us who are in the postal service. I'm on the beat to serve you, not be your friend—so to speak. Friendly, yes. Relationship—well, not so readily approved by the United States postal people. Can't stop to chat. The mailman doesn't ring twice, and all that."

"So . . . it was ok for me to approach you, but not for you to approach me, is that what you're saying?"

"Something like that. I probably should have laughed off your invitation and continued with the way things were . . . but frankly, I knew you had stopped seeing Ian and I was relieved about that, and I figured if there ever was an opening for getting to know the adult Molly Herman, last night was it."

"How did you know I had ever even dated Ian?"

"He told me," said Peter. "Didn't mean to, but he did. He said one day that he had met a great gal—beautiful but really down to earth, accomplished and straightforward, but with a lot of depth, and then he told me you lived on Elm Street. Said your name was Molly. That pretty much brought everything into sharp focus."

"Aha," said Molly.

Peter continued, "The truth was, I initially had suggested that he try to get to know you."

"You WHAT?"

"We were at Grams one day, which was really not all that usual, and when I asked about Sterilyn he said they had parted ways and he was pretty bummed about being without a woman in his life. Said he was looking for less glamour and more substance. I told him there was a single woman in my neighborhood who was an excellent combination of both good looks and substance. He asked your name. I told him he'd have to do any further sleuthing on his own. But I did tell him that your neighborhood was having a neighborhood meeting in a couple of days and he should attend and see what he could see."

"That's where we met," admitted Molly softly, putting together pieces as if working a jigsaw. "He asked me out for coffee after the meeting, and for some very odd reason, I didn't ask him where he lived. I didn't realize for almost a month that he really didn't live in my neighborhood at all. When I asked him what he had been doing at the meeting he said, 'Looking for you.' I thought that was just a nice line, and frankly, I was glad we had found each other—at that point."

Peter didn't say anything, and Molly forged ahead to fill the void, "So you were the set-up guy."

"Yeah," Peter said softly. "I guess you could put it that way. Frankly, I didn't think it would last as long as it did. I figured you might eventually figure out he was Lyman. Maybe, just maybe, he'd mention that he had been in your childhood and so had I. At the bare minimum, I thought I might learn a little more about you—the adult you—but Ian only talked in broad generalities. Ian has always been pretty shallow, in my opinion, and I really didn't think he'd be able to hang on to you. I thought you'd dump him after several dates. It was a huge surprise, let me assure you, that you hung in there as long as you did."

"Truth told, he dumped *me*," said Molly.

"Perhaps," said Peter. "I think Ian knew he was in over his head—that he might really fall for you and that you'd eventually see through him and the crash would be fierce. It says something, don't you think that he never put two and two together and came up with Molly of Herman's Pond?"

"Suppose so," said Molly. "On the other hand, what does it say that I didn't recognize him as Lyman?"

They both laughed—but it was a little hollow.

"I was bedazzled, I admit," said Molly, "that he was so far up a social ladder I had never even imagined climbing. He didn't seem to have any money worries, or for that matter, any kind of worries. He lived far more carefree than I have ever lived, or can ever imagine living. It was a bit intoxicating—no alcohol involved."

"It's his veneer," said Peter. "He has money worries. Like how much longer his father is going to put up with his having an office and a brass plaque on his desk without ever doing any work of value to the company. Worries like how much Grams is going to continue to dish out of his trust fund before she dies . . . and God forbid, whether she might change her will. Grams has an eye for quality and depth, and I suspect at times that for all Ian's charm, he comes up lacking in her eyes. Ian's worries are ones he could do something about . . . but he's been pampered for so many years now, it's hard to imagine what might jolt him into the real world. His two sisters are just the same."

"I never met them."

"Doubted that you ever would. They live back east and that's mostly so the rest of the family won't know how they are living, or with whom. That side of the family doesn't bring much joy to the rest of us. I don't mind saying at all, as we sit here on this side of the new year, that I'm glad you and Ian are history."

"It sorta hurt, however, that he went back to Sterilyn in such a quick turnabout," said Molly. "I didn't even know she was still in the picture."

"She wasn't, I don't think, for a while at least," said Peter. "But the guy she was seeing turned out to be a crook—a major crook, not just a minor player—and I don't think she could see herself waiting out a prison term. As for Ian . . . well, Sterilyn's family has so much money that it makes the Glossman coffers look meager—and she's an only child."

"I didn't know about the money," Molly said.

"It makes it a bit easier, doesn't it?" Peter replied.

"Yes, I think it does," said Molly. "It puts a depth level on shallow, at least!"

"Good," said Peter. "And that's all the time I want to devote to discussing Lyman on this bright new year, new day."

"There's something else I really want to know, however," said Molly.

"About Lyman?"

"No, about you."

"Okay."

"Why are you a postman?"

"Mind if we discuss it over a walk tomorrow afternoon? I hear it is supposed to be a rare fifty-degree day." Looking at his watch he added, "It's six o'clock and I'm supposed to be at a friend's house in half an hour for a traditional homage to college football. Our mutually-supported team isn't in the game, but the team that beat us *is*, so we find ourselves rooting for the opposition that has now become 'our side.' An odd sort of arrangement, I think.

"Anyway, kick-off is pending and while I know that might sound incredibly shallow—it *is* a once-a-year celebration at which my attendance is required. And unfortunately, knowing you for only one very full and wonderful day doesn't quite qualify you yet for a fifty-yard seat on the sofa in the media room. The questions would be endless—both spoken and unspoken—and I don't want to put you through all that. Not to mention the fact that there will be food—and I know that I can sidestep that one, but as a new kid on the sofa, you'd be hard-pressed to say 'no' and that wouldn't be fair . . . or healthy."

"Me thinks you explain too much," Molly laughed with a mock take on Shakespeare.

"Maybe."

"I am grateful for the bit about your concern for my gastro-intestinal track." Molly added. *What? I'm talking to my mailman about my gastro-intestinal track . . . and it makes sense?* Molly liked football but the very idea of meeting Peter's circle of friends was a bit daunting. She had barely met Peter!

Then, very seriously, Peter Lorgham looked into her eyes and said, "I like you too much, Molly Herman, to go so fast that I derail this train on its tracks. But . . . I would like to go for that walk tomorrow afternoon."

"Deal," she said. "I'm glad for an evening of quiet to sort out some to-do lists." *And call Tams!*

So much had happened in just six hours!

9

"Your new guy Peter is Petie-Eye!" Tams exclaimed so loudly that Molly had to move the receiver away from her ear.

"And not only that," Molly quickly added. "The famous Ian Glossman is actually . . . drumroll and don't pass out . . . Lyman."

"Lyman?"

"Lyman—the one from when we were seven or eight or nine years old."

"LYMAN?"

"Right."

"Noooooo."

"Yep."

"Weird . . . are you sure?"

Molly recounted her BBQ lunch with Peter almost verbatim.

"And you tell me that Peter has a master of science degree from State and he's your postman? What's with that?"

"I don't know. I asked him pointblank, 'Why are you a postman?' and he suggested we go for a walk tomorrow afternoon."

"Is the weather there warm enough for a walk?"

"Strangely so," Molly said. "I'm not going to let him be evasive. Something isn't quite connecting here and I need to find out what it is."

"Actually," noted Tams, "something seems to be very much connecting here—and a few things in very surprising ways. And for that reason, you really DO need to find out about it."

"You're right."

"And then call me and tell me!"

Molly promised . . . slept well . . . awoke early and with a strong desire to attend early church . . . came home and fixed herself Eggs Benedict . . . took a little nap . . . and felt altogether refreshed inside and out when Peter called at two o'clock.

"Do you have on your walking shoes?" he asked brightly.

"Sure do."

"I'm there in ten," he said.

And he was. This time in the red pick-up. "I felt the need to convince you that the pick-up was real."

"Where shall we walk?" Molly asked as she tossed a scarf around her neck.

"I thought we might walk right here in your neighborhood."

"But you do that five times a week, at least when you aren't in your little post office vehicle."

"Yes," said Peter. "But you don't know my route. I thought you might want to walk a mile in my shoes."

"I do," said Molly. "I have no idea what your route includes."

If she could have read Peter's mind, she would found him thinking, *You have THAT right.*

They headed east, which ended several hundred yards away in a cul-de-sac. Shortly after they left Molly's driveway, she said, "So . . . why *are* you a mailman?"

Peter smiled. He liked her tenacity and direct approach. She felt his "like."

"When I got out of college, I worked in a regular corporate job for awhile. But frankly, I felt like I was becoming stuck—like a mushroom growing on the underside of a log. I needed to move more, get outdoors more, see more, do more. I felt as if the office was a closed world when it came to people—the clients that came through the door were interesting, but their arrival was sporadic. I was stuck with the people with whom I worked, and although they tended to be a rather ambitious lot, their conversation was limited to what they owned, where they had been clubbing the night before, or in some cases, what they were investing in and how much antacid their doctor was now prescribing. Most of what they talked about apart from work projects was a real bore."

"Sounds terrible," Molly noted, mentally appraising her own work situation. "Perhaps it was just that particular office?"

"Perhaps. But it was my particular office and I wanted out of it. So I did a quick inventory of what it was that I wanted in a job—not just the big goals, but the daily to-do list."

"And what did you come up with."

"Four big things."

"Four. Sounds as if you really thought it out."

"I did. First, I wanted a job that had plenty of 'outside' to it. I didn't need to be in the forest or out on a New Mexico plateau, but I needed to be out in the elements of fresh air and changing scenery . . . ."

"And changing weather."

"That, too. I like the changing seasons, and I like the fact that the weather in this part of the country can change on a dime. There's a certain dynamic to that . . . and I like it."

"Number two?"

He's so organized. Analytical. Molly was intrigued.

"Number two was that I wanted something that was a little physical. I've never been one for going to a gym for exercise—that has always seemed a bit artificial to me. I wanted a job where I got in enough exercise just doing the work that was before me to do. Walking the route of a mail carrier is good exercise on two accounts—the walking, and also the lifting and carrying of the bag, which I don't do always, but which I do enough of. I usually walk about six miles a day in this job. Even at a rather slow pace, that's good exercise."

"Okay—outside job, plenty of fresh air and exercise. Number three?"

"Number three—meeting people I wouldn't otherwise meet."

Molly felt herself blushing slightly.

"People who weren't in your regular social circle," she noted simply.

"Well, yes, I guess, although I didn't come at it from that angle," Peter said. "Not just my social circle, as you call it, but general society segments. You'd be amazed at who lives in your neighborhood and what they all do. Do you know your neighbors?"

Molly gave the question a little thought before answering. She knew a few names—the Davis family next door, in the dry cleaning business; the Walsh family across the street, he was a banker; the Stewards on the other side, he was a pediatrician. But know them socially? Personally? Not really. She had been to a neighborhood meeting or two, and had stopped in briefly for a couple of backyard parties. That didn't add to much interaction, or much relationship.

"No, I really don't know my neighbors."

"Do you know who lives in that house?" Peter asked, pointing to a rather pinkish ranch style house, circa 1950s with wrought iron ornamentation around the front porch.

"No," admitted Molly.

"Her name is Helene. Her husband was a general in the army. They traveled the world— military bases and then, later in his career, on assignments that were more diplomatic than war-related. Left her exhausted after a decade or so, so she decided to stay home. He died about ten years ago and she threw herself into a book club and the local ballet organization. Various groups of gals meet for lunch once a month or so, and she does the organizing, book choosing, cooking, and general entertaining. It's her life."

Molly found it interesting that *Peter* seemed so interested.

"The problem is that she lives alone and her two sons are out of state and hardly ever call or visit. She's a lonely person. And she's not all that steady on her feet. I promised her that I would ring the bell every day as I put the mail through the front door slot, and I asked her to let me know she was okay by waving to me from a window or door as I crossed the street to drop off mail and then walked back toward her house and the cart. She does that every day."

"That's really wonderful of you," Molly said glancing at the house's windows as they walked back past the pink brick house.

"One day she didn't wave. Her car was there, but no lights were on. I called her on my cell phone and thank God I did. She had fallen in the night, had barely made it back to her bedside, crawling in pain all the way, and she was curled up on the floor but able to pull the phone off the end table when it rang. She was so rattled that she couldn't remember what number to call for help. We got her an ambulance and she came home from several weeks of hip surgery recovery and rehab . . . three days before Christmas."

"Should she be living alone?" Molly asked.

"No. I have encouraged her to check out various options and her sons are coming later this week. She may not be your neighbor much longer— my push is for the new senior living center down on Warren Avenue."

Molly nodded. "I have a hunch you could tell me stories of every person on this block," she finally said as they rounded a bend to take a side street.

"Most. Not all. Some people aren't home during the day, but plenty are. I only have a chance to speak to some of them—maybe not more than a hundred words a month, but there's a little connection, I think. They know I care. They know I'm aware. And mostly, they know I'm there."

"Hey, it's a poem." Molly laughed. "Care, aware, there."

Peter replied quickly, "Don't you DARE. It would be a SCARE for you to think I'm a poet."

"Who lives *there*?" Molly asked as they passed a house with a significant amount of overgrowth in the front beds.

"A man named Carvill. That's his first name, I think. Actually, it might be his last name. Most of the mail that comes here comes to Occupant, or just to "Carvill, esq." Nobody else has *that* title on this route, trust me. He used to own a car dealership. He spends most of his time at Lake Howell. Has a houseboat there, but lets all his mail pile up here. He told me just last week that he thinks he may sell this place, as is. Said he just doesn't care about a yard or home upkeep anymore."

"That's pretty obvious."

"And even the timers on lights aren't all that much of a visual deterrent, I suspect. The house sends a big message, 'nobody is here.' He told me would rather live on his houseboat than on land and asked me about mail delivery to a houseboat."

"Do you know how much he wants for his house?"

"No. But I'm guessing a buyer could have it at a very good price, and if the buyer was willing to do some upgrading, it might make for a good flip."

Peter was a wellspring of information about Molly's neighbors and she couldn't help but be intrigued with all he knew.

"Ever notice that the Christmas decorations have never been taken down from that house," he asked, pointing to a house at the end of another cul-de-sac in the neighborhood.

"Not really," said Molly, "In fact, I'm not sure I have ever even seen this house. I never drive down this street. Does anybody live there?"

"Mail is picked up daily," said Peter. "Came one day to find the garage door open. Walls are lined with boxes of all sizes and shapes. The neighbor to the west told me that UPS makes almost daily deliveries and pickups."

"Aha! The competition," said Molly.

"Don't tell anybody, but I use 'em, too. And frankly, if the dweller in this house is generating as much box traffic as the neighbor says, I'm glad not to be toting all those boxes."

"What do you think is going on?"

"The neighbor didn't know for sure but thinks the owner uses the house as an office—and enjoys swimming in the pool out back. Seems to leave about five to five-thirty every night, is there before nine in the morning."

"What kind of business?"

"Not sure," said Peter. "I'm hoping it's just a multi-level business—soap, vitamins, plastics, that sort of thing. Neighbor didn't know."

"I'm betting it's a guy owner," said Molly. "A woman wouldn't want all those decorations gathering that much dust."

"Actually," said Peter, "the neighbor said she thinks the owner is a woman—at least the few glimpses she has caught led her to think that. Owner's car has tinted windows and owner always wears a hat of some kind."

"Hmmm, the plot thickens."

"There's a place just over the back fence of that house," said Peter, "that definitely has a plot thickening." He laughed.

"Okay," said Molly, "there's a joke there I'm not getting."

"Yes there is, and don't tell," said Peter, "because I want this news to come from me to the police in a few weeks. The guy is growing a plot of pot in his backyard."

"Noooo," said Molly. "I live in a drug neighborhood?"

"Afraid so. Lovely *Cannabis sativa* plants. He was unloading a tray of seedlings one day when I delivered his mail."

"What did you do?"

"I said, 'Hey, Mr. Epstein, great little hemp plants you have there.'"

"And he said?"

"He answered me with robust cheer, 'I hear they make a great hedge.'"

"Do you think he truly didn't know what he had purchased and was about to plant?"

"Not sure. On the other hand, his twenty-year-old grandson—complete with tattoos and piercings—has been helping him in his hothouse and yard and I suspect *he* is fully knowledgeable about what his grandfather is growing."

"Why wait a few weeks?"

"Closer to harvest. More evidence."

And so it went.

Molly learned who were the best gardeners . . . and who were the best cooks. Peter apparently was given the occasional bouquet to "take home to your sweetheart" or the occasional casserole to "give your sweetheart a night away from cooking chores."

"And what does your sweetheart say?" asked Molly.

"Geez, you are as bad as they are," said Peter. "Intent on fishing to see if I have a sweetheart and what she might be like!"

"Speaking of food, what do you say we head back to my house and I'll heat up some of my fabulous holiday leftovers for you."

"Sounds great. But before we turn around, I want you to take note of that house with the semi-tudor architecture."

"The one with grey trim?"

"Right."

"What about it?"

"No matter what anybody may ever say to you, don't go in that house."

Molly was a bit alarmed at the rather serious tone of Peter's voice. "The bogey man lives there?" she asked lightly.

"Just promise me. No matter who may call to you from the door, or engage you in the yard . . . and no matter what they might want you to see, or offer to give you 'free for the taking,' do *not* go into that house. In fact, don't even go up on the porch close enough to the door that you could be shoved or pulled into that house."

"You're serious."

"Very," said Peter. "Promise me."

"Okay," said Molly. "I promise. But you need to give me a little more reason to stay away, I think . . . Are you just trying to see if I scare easily?"

"No," said Peter, flatly. "I'm not kidding about this. There's reason to be fearful." And he left it at that, picking up his pace with a challenge, "Last one back for leftovers gets what's left over!"

10

Back at her house, Molly began pulling things from her refrigerator and setting them on the counter for selection. "Instant buffet," said Molly.

"An opportunity for creative dining," added Peter.

Together they concocted a rather elaborate and exotic salad to go with bowls of chicken-corn chowder, homemade and ready for reheating.

"Sometimes leftovers are the best," said Peter. "But the greater truth, I think, is that when leftovers are recombined, they create something entirely *new*, and in lots of cases, the new is better than the old."

Molly had a vague sense that he was talking about her and their budding relationship and possibly the recent demise of her relationship with Ian and perhaps the end of some sort of relationship in his life . . . but she didn't want to read too much into his words.

"So now," she said, "what's reason number four that you are a mailman."

"You're good," said Peter. "Great memory and lots of tenacity."

"You've got that right."

"Information," he said simply. "I like to learn new things and the people on this particular route know a lot of interesting things."

"Like what?" Molly asked.

"Well, from a guy named Fred I get regular stock tips. He thinks I'm a day trader in my night hours. He's always clueing me in to something— some of which just may be insider trading. I smile and nod and then once a week or so I call my broker and ask him to investigate the companies Fred tells me about. I let the broker do the deciding and dealing, but let's just leave it at this, Fred has made me some money."

"Are you a day trader?" Molly asked.

"No, but I do stay up with the market. I have a portfolio that I consider to be a management responsibility in my life."

Molly didn't reply. She had figured as much. The limo and country club were not artificial plumage. She had known that within ten minutes of arrival at the club.

"Are you so rich that being a mailman is a hobby?"

"I won't lie to you by either commission or omission, Molly. I have money. Not enough to be in the financial stratosphere, but certainly enough that I don't need to work as a mailman. On the other hand, I am not at all interested in sitting around and doing nothing. I play a good game of golf and an occasional genius game of handball, but I have no desire to sit at the club after eighteen holes every day talking about which shots were good and which were bad. I like working . . . and I like the work I do."

Molly nodded and then asked, "What other kinds of information do you get from my neighbors?"

"Some of the information isn't put into words. I can tell from the occasional campaign yard signs who stands for what, and who supports whom. I can tell from the mail what people are into—those who get lots of junk mail and catalogs related to animals are probably people who have pets, those who are into ski resorts and winter clothing are probably those who love to go skiing. It isn't rocket science, but it's interesting."

"And I'll bet you know all the dogs and cats in the neighborhood."

"On a first-name basis!" Peter said quickly. "I get along with them all and they sometimes have their own stories to tell."

"I'm sure," Molly laughed. "And of course you can probably tell when people have birthdays by the cards that show up."

"Usually. It's a bit tough for those who have birthdays close to Christmas. But yes, I do know your birthday is probably in early August sometime."

"The eighth." Molly blushed a little. "Hold that thought."

"I also have a little idea about the dynamics of the relationships in some of the houses. I know that Sam and Jon are just roommates, not lovers, as their neighbors on both sides think. I know that Marge and Ann are lovers, and not roommates. Also not what their neighbors think. I know that the kids in one house are latch-key and are up to some things their parents likely don't know about, but also likely wouldn't care about if informed. The kids are quick to throw their unfinished cans of beer over into adjacent yards. I know that there's one couple that likely didn't survive the holidays as a couple—I've walked up to their door to hear too many loud and angry exchanges. And there were no signs of decorating this year."

"What other things besides my birth month do you think you know about me?" Molly asked.

"I know that you probably have a very good credit rating since you get a lot of mail asking you to add one more credit card to your wallet, and you get no 'second notice' mailings that tell me your electricity or natural gas are about to be cut off.

"I also know that you like things related to home-making and decorating, at least if the home-related gift catalogs and magazines are a good clue. From some of the mail, I gather that you enjoy cooking and like manhandling cooking gadgets. Of course, I now know that from personal experience, not just from the mail!"

Before Molly could say anything, he continued, "I know that you must do some of your clothes shopping by catalog. And I suspect you have been on a cruise at some point, or would like to go on a cruise—given the cruise line notices and brochures.

"I know where you went to college, given the alumni mailings.

"I know that you still dream of winning the Publisher's Clearinghouse Sweepstakes, and that you likely attend the Philharmonic concerts, the opera, and the musical theater series at the performing-arts center—or would like to, or have in the past."

"You're a little scary, Peter Lorgham," Molly finally interjected. "Kinda like a stalker without stalking."

"One big difference," Peter said.

"What's that?"

"What I *don't* know about you is far more intriguing than what I do know. The stuff you can learn from observation of a person's house, car, mail, and general neighborhood demeanor is like a filter. Clears away the riff-raff. First round of hurdles. Baseline information. I know the people in this neighborhood that I *don't* need to know beyond our current 'professional relationship.' And in your case, I see a person that I'd like to get to know a lot better."

"I'm glad," said Molly. "And I feel as if I'm behind. You know far more about me than I know about you."

"Ask me your questions, I'll tell you no lies."

"It's a deal!"

While they cleared away the dishes and food, Molly asked. "You need to tell me what's with the grey-trimmed house you ordered me to stay out of. What do you know?"

"I can't tell you everything I know," Peter said softly. Then he added, "Let's just say that I know it's bad, but I don't know fully how bad. I'm still trying to determine that."

"A mystery."

"Something like that." And then he said brightly, "Much as I'd like to stay here long into the evening, I need to get home to pack."

Molly glanced at the clock and was surprised to see it was already 6:30. "Pack?" she asked. "Are you going on a nice long exotic cruise through the waters of the Caribbean?"

"Hardly. Although the idea sounds very appealing. Business trip. I don't know exactly when I'll be back—could be two or three days, could be a week. But I'll check in with you, if that's acceptable to you?"

"I'd like that."

It was only after Peter walked out her front door and she saw Houndcat staring up at her with a quizzical tilt of his head that she found herself saying aloud, "What kind of *business* does a postman fly away to do?"

And then, as after-burner questions, "Or, is it financial business? And what made me think he was flying? And why doesn't he know when he's returning?"

11

"Those are just the beginning of *my* questions!" Tams said. "Petie-Eye has turned out to be a man of mystery. I'm thinking that maybe I need to fly there to meet him . . . or maybe we should say, meet him again . . . adult terms."

"That would be tantamount to my taking him home to meet my parents, Tams. We're no place close to that yet. I wasn't even at that point with Ian."

"Good thing. They probably would have recognized immediately that he was Lyman and would have wondered if you were in your right mind."

"Which I apparently wasn't. I think that's one of the reasons I want to ask Peter so many questions. He doesn't seem to mind, but I really don't want to come across as the MC of the Miss 20 Questions Show. I just didn't ask Ian enough questions."

"Don't beat yourself up about it."

"No," said Molly. "But I'm eager to see if Peter calls this week—and eager to see if I'm fully able to concentrate on my very long list of things to do both at work and home."

"You'll be fine. I'm here any time you have a scoop to share."

"Right. This week is devoted to regrouping— making lists, restocking the pantry, sorting out a closet or two. I'll stay busy."

The next afternoon after work she stopped by Wilson's—the new upscale natural-foods grocery that had opened a couple of miles from her home.

Molly wasn't prepared to see Ian in the produce section. He was surveying the bundles of fresh cilantro and nearly ran into her with his cart.

"Oops, sorry," he said, and then added a little too loudly and too cheerfully as he recognized the woman he had nearly run over, "Molly!"

"Ian," she replied, and seeing what he was putting into his cart, she couldn't help but blurt out. "Do you know what to do with cilantro?"

"Not really," he said. But then holding out a list, added, "It's just on the list. I'm doing what I was told to do."

Molly suddenly had a rash idea and barreled headlong into it. "By the way, I didn't see you at the ball on New Year's Eve."

He didn't seem to mind, or perhaps didn't remember that he should mind. "Nope. Missed that gig. Was out of town."

"It was a true extravaganza. Thanks again for the tickets. I went with somebody you know."

"Really? Who would that be?"

"Your cousin Peter."

"Lorgham?"

"Right."

"How on earth did you meet Peter? I didn't even know he was still in town."

"Why wouldn't he be?" said Molly. "Being a mailman is a pretty regular stay-in-town sort of job."

"Peter's a mailman?" Ian asked.

"Guess you aren't that close," Molly said, a little surprised at the genuine tone of Ian's question.

"Guess not," said Ian. "I thought he was working for the government a little higher up on the food chain."

"Well, enjoy your cilantro," Molly said. "See you around."

"Yeah, right," said Ian.

He never was very good at ending things—not even a conversation in the vegetable department, thought Molly.

As she drove home she pondered new questions:

Why didn't Ian know Peter was working as a mailman? He had obviously been at the job long enough to have thoroughly cased her neighborhood.

What did Ian mean by the phrase "working for the government a little higher up on the food chain"?

Peter called two nights later. "This trip has taken a couple of odd twists and turns. I probably won't be back in town until early next week."

Molly asked, "Where are you lolling about?"

He laughed. "No lolling. But I am missing you."

"Same here."

She was glad he had called. Her questions could be asked later.

Molly decided that part of what she wanted to do while Peter was away was do a little more walking in her neighborhood. It was a way of relating—sorta, tangentially, secretly. It would be good exercise. *And who knows,* she thought, *I might have some new information for him when he returns!*

12

"What are you going to let me tell her?" Peter asked.

"Who?" asked Lance, as he casually reached for the container holding sugar and sweeteners in an array of pastel colors.

"Molly."

"Molly, who?" asked Lance, honestly clueless.

"Tams' best friend from childhood," Peter said in a chiding tone.

"You're kidding!" Lance replied. "You're in touch with *that* Molly?"

"In touch," said Lance. "Perhaps in relationship."

"But I thought we agreed that you wouldn't go there—at least not until the current project has ended."

"Well . . ." said Peter, "I think it's more that you told me you didn't think it was a good idea for me to look her up. I don't recall anything about not talking to her. As for 'looking her up,' kinda difficult, don't you think when she's on my mail route."

"Talking to her—in your official role as an employee of the United States Postal Service—is a far cry from being in touch with her . . . or in relationship . . . and certainly a far cry from wanting to divulge information to her," said Lance, suddenly animated, but lowering his voice, suddenly aware that people in adjacent booths at Mike's Café might overhear.

"You're acting as if I rang her bell and said, 'Hi, here's your mail and I'm an acquaintance from your past and I'm working with your best friend

Tams' husband and oh, by the way, would you like to go out?" Peter said, leaning over the Formica table and lowering his voice to Lance's level.

"Well, if that wasn't the case, what *was* the case?"

"She asked me to the country club ball that was held on New Year's Eve."

"She asked *you*?"

"Yep." said Peter. "Met me at the door and said, and I quote, 'Would you like to go to a New Year's Eve party with me?'"

"You're kidding."

"Nope."

"Doesn't sound like the Molly I know. But then again, the right answer to her question would have been, 'No, but thank you anyway.'"

"I was surprised—caught off guard a bit. Besides, do you really know this woman? I know you met her years ago and I know you probably know *some* things from what Tams has said about her. But let me tell you, from my perspective, she's the finest woman I've met in the last ten years, maybe in my entire life."

"And you know all this since New Year's Eve?" said Lance, looking at his watch as if to say, *Not a long time, buddy.*

"I've been delivering her mail for months. You can learn a lot about a person by delivering their mail, and by seeing how a person lives—in an overall, coming and going, planting and mowing, driving by, curtains open sort of way."

"You sound like a stalker," Lance said, lowering his voice to almost a whisper.

"Not at all. You just observe and you just know. Hey—that is our business, isn't it? At least seventy-plus percent of it, I'd guess."

Lance looked away, pausing for the waitress to set down his order of pancakes and Peter's omelet.

"More coffee when you get a chance," he said to her.

Then, turning to Peter he said, "Yes, observation is a big part of what we do. Of course it is. And right now, I'm observing the situation and I'm concluding that this *could* be a problem, but not necessarily. How much does she know?"

"About?"

"About you. About your life, your job, the project."

"She knows that I knew her as a kid, but frankly, she is several years younger so all of that work on my grandfather's ranch is purely innocent history. She has no idea about the role of the ranch in the last five years.

"And," Peter continued, "she knows that I have three cars, that I am a member of the country club, and that I have a very wealthy grandmother— whom she met during the time she was dating my cousin Ian. She's been in Grams' home and she knows . . . ."

"Hold everything. She knows Ian?"

"She dated him for several months. It ended when Sterilyn came back to town."

"Does she know Sterilyn?"

"Only by reputation, and perhaps sight recognition at a distance—at least as far as I know."

"Nothing about Sterilyn's 'trouble?'" Lance asked, again reducing the volume of his voice to a whisper.

"Don't think so."

"Back to what she knows . . . ."

"She knows I work for the USPS and we have walked some of my route," said Peter, and seeing the rise in Lance's eyebrows, he quickly added, "It was a sunny day, good for a walk, and we walked. Nothing more. She knows that I invest in the stock market and am a caring guy for some of her neighbors and that's it. She knows nothing of the project."

"And why does she think her mailman happens to be in Alexandria?"

"She doesn't know where I am," said Peter. "Nobody does except you, me, and the bosses that be."

"She doesn't know what's on your badge?"

"No."

"In your walk-about, did you go by Gray Tudor?" Lance asked.

"Yes."

"Did you say anything to her about Gray Tudor?"

"I told her I thought it was a place she should steer clear of."

"And you don't think that would make her more curious?"

"No, she's got plenty to think about without thinking about Gray Tudor."

"And you think she'll steer clear?"

"Yes."

"So what is it that you want to tell her?"

"I want a really really—and did I say *really*—good excuse about why a normal street-beat mailman is called away on business and doesn't return for . . . how long did you say it might be?"

"It could be two or three weeks. From here, you'll be going to Portland."

"As in Oregon or Maine?"

"Oregon."

"And after that I return to the mailman beat?"

"Depends on what happens in Oregon."

"Back to my question, 'What can I tell her? What's my good excuse?'"

Lance gave a big sigh, took his last bite of syrup-dripping pancake, and said, "I don't know if you'll be going back to the mailman beat."

"Why not?"

"Well, the complicating factor here is not Molly. It's the fact that this is your home city. You are known there. You are identifiable in a number of ways. You—and we—don't want any of your family to ever know what has gone down, or be in any kind of danger. And now, that includes Molly. Unless we can make serious headway and wrap up this particular situation pretty soon—and without any clue whatsoever that you have been involved, you may not have a future with Molly—at least not where she lives right now."

Peter sat back in the booth and stared out the window at the traffic out on the street.

"And what happens if I bail out now?"

"You could do that," Lance said. "But I know you. You won't. We're too close to a big take-down."

Peter continued to stare out the window.

"I think I have an idea, however," said Lance, "about the excuse you can give Molly. Ah man . . . Molly! Tams' friend. Who would have thought? . . . ."

"Speaking of which, my turn to ask a question or two," said Peter.

"Fire away."

"Does Tams know about me?"

"She knows I'm working on a project with a guy named William who goes by Liam."

"Interesting," said Peter. To be sure, his first name *was* William. William Peter Lorgham. "I like the name Liam. Wish I had thought to use it."

"Nobody would have understood it twenty-five years ago," Lance said. He paused for a moment of reflection. *Liam and Ian . . . too close . . . I could have been the one called Lyman!*

"So, I'm Liam. Pleased to meet you," Peter said. "Next question—have you ever mentioned anything about the Sterilyn case to Tams?"

"No. Well, at least not directly. I have dubbed her Bait. Tams knows that's not her real name, and she thinks its funny. She knows the case has to do with a bait-and-switch scam that involves some really bad guys. I never tell any details. What I do tell is enough to give Tams full assurance that she and the girls are safe and they don't need to worry about me."

"So she has no idea that I'm in town partly to give a deposition related to the former boyfriend of a woman named Bait?"

"No idea."

"Good."

"Well, good, and not so good. I'm going to have to come up with an excuse, too."

"For what?"

"For explaining just why I can't invite my new colleague named Liam over for dinner."

"What's she cooking?" Peter asked with a grin.

"Barbecue spare ribs and her famous almost-Chinese rice."

"Oh man!" said Peter. "Barbecue."

"Yeah," said Lance. "She hasn't cooked it in a long time but just last week, she said that's what she was going to cook this coming weekend. Said it was the sauce she used to eat at a restaurant when she was a kid."

"Miller's?" Peter asked.

"Yeah," said Lance, "you know what she's talking about?"

"It was a place we all went as kids," said Peter. "You're right. Liam can't show up at dinner. I'm not sure I could play that dumb, and I'm not sure *she* wouldn't start putting pieces together."

"So . . . I'll tell her that you have other plans."

"Tell her I had to fly to Maine."

"Maine?"

"Yeah, the other Portland. You've got nicknames for everything, make that the name for my next home away from home."

"Good idea."

"And now, let's hear your really *really* REALLY good excuse for Molly."

13

Molly answered the phone on the first ring. She had been eager to hear from Peter and she didn't care if he knew it.

"Hey, mailman, where's my mail?" she asked breezily.

"What, my colleagues are failing you?" he said, with an equally light-hearted tone.

"Oh, the mail's fine," Molly said with a sigh. "I just miss my regular mailman."

"Glad to be missed," Peter said.

"Any idea when you'll be home from your secret mission?" Molly asked. "I have a killer recipe for artichoke dip that I'd like to try out on you."

"Wish I could," said Peter, thinking but not saying, *Oh, how I wish I could*. It was a little unnerving that she had used the phrase "secret mission," and then, in the very next sentence, the word "killer."

Quickly realizing that he hadn't really answered her question, Peter added, "This could take awhile."

"But the post office has done so much improving lately on its quick delivery of the mail!"

Peter smiled. Banter with Molly was always quick-witted. He liked that immensely.

"Are you going to tell me that they're promoting you to Postmaster General?" Molly added.

Peter laughed. "You know, I've never really understand the use of the word 'General' for the top boss of the United States Postal Service. Do you suppose it has something to do with the Revolutionary War, or maybe the Civil War?"

Molly smiled. Banter with Peter was fun and casual and very oh-so-relational. She liked all three qualities . . . immensely.

"If you're being promoted to general, I'll salute," said Molly, "but I won't really like the idea. I do, however, like a man in uniform!"

If she only knew, Peter said.

The truth was oh so close . . . the truth he didn't dare tell Molly. He was a man with a uniform—regular, combat camo, and full dress. He knew that she'd like it if he told her that, so he did and then added, "Every guy has got to have three kinds of clothes—to go with his three cars."

Ah, the truth . . . .

Peter and Lance had first met when they were both in the military. First Iraq conflict. In Kuwait. Both of them fighter pilots. Both using their planes to do more than patrol northern air space.

After their deployment had ended, they had found themselves in D.C.—being offered civilian assignments in keeping with their espionage abilities. Lance, C.I.A. and Peter, F.B.I.

In Kuwait, they both had mutually admitted that they *thought* they might have met in the past. The admission came in the expanded mess hall during a Thanksgiving Day meal. In comparing totally unclassified college experiences, they realized they had been in the same place at the same time. Lance had been Army. Peter had been Navy. And they had met in the skybox of a mutual friend at the big Army-Navy showdown game.

Lance was married to Tams by then, but barely so. Peter had commented on her name when he was introduced to her, had been told its origin by Tams herself, and had even been told that Molly had given her the name. "Clever girl," Peter had said. Tams had agreed . . . "and beautiful, and smart, and very kind. Maybe you should meet her! Although I'm not sure how she'd feel about a Navy man."

"And what's wrong with Navy?" Peter had asked, "Apart from the fact that you had the unfortunate fate to fall for an Army guy?"

"Well," Tams had said with a hint of flirtation—made possible because Lance had been at her elbow, "what's wrong with a Navy man is that they are losers . . . at least, that's what the scoreboard will say in about two hours."

They all had laughed. It had been friendly enough banter. And if truth be known, Peter wasn't at all sure Navy could pull out the game. He had gone on to ask Tams several other questions and it confirmed his previous math equation—two and two really did add up to four in this case. He had made very certain that he had revealed nothing about his own childhood history or the city of his residence. Even then, he knew enough to disclose only what was absolutely essential. But, he had gone home feeling intrigued by the encounter . . . and wondering just a bit about what kind of woman Tams' friend Molly had turned out to be.

When Peter's superiors had partnered him with Lance a little over a year ago, he had felt a genuine moment of what he called "full-circle-ism." And when the new assignment that put them together turned out to be based in Peter's home city, and his assignment as a postman included walking Molly's neighborhood, a tremendous sense of fatalism had taken root—not fatalism in the sense of "resignation to what might be impending disaster," but rather, a sense that "what *should* be, is unfolding as it *should* be." That had been Grams' definition of fatalism and he had always liked it.

Now, here he was, about to lie to that very same Molly.

"Wow. I never thought about the uniform possibilities," he said. "This could be a good thing!"

"You're evading the issue," Molly said.

"You are right," said Peter. "Partly because I don't know the answer."

"Not even part of an answer?" Molly asked.

"Well," began Peter, clearly with the thought, *I've got to remember this bit of fiction I'm about to tell* . . . "I'm being asked to do something that the United States Postal Service apparently thinks I'm perfectly capable of doing, although how exactly they determined that I'm the *perfect* guy for the job is a bit of a stretch, as far as I'm concerned."

"Hmmm. Perfect guy," Molly mused aloud. "I sorta get that, but perfect guy for what job exactly?"

"It's more of a project than a full-time job," Peter said, stalling for time.

"Okay, this project you're being asked to do . . ." conceded "This project is . . ."

"Is to put in place a national protocol for determining greater on-the job efficiency for us mailmen." *Jiminy . . . is she going to buy this?* Peter wasn't at all sure.

"On the job efficiency?"

"Yeah . . . combining some routes, eliminating others, remapping routes, determining if delivery by cart or foot is better, factoring in the idea of neighborhood banks of mailboxes. That sort of thing."

"Well, I can tell you right now that I absolutely hate the idea of neighborhood banks of mailboxes," Molly said.

"Duly noted."

"Big question," Molly said. *Here it comes . . . she's going to tell me that she knows I'm lying.*

"Shoot," said Peter, immediately grimacing to himself at his choice of word.

"How is it that a mailman who delivers mail in my quiet and obscure little neighborhood gets tapped for a national efficiency project, and why can't that national efficiency project have its 'home office' right here in our home town?"

"That's two questions."

"Take 'em one at a time, Lorgham," Molly said in a third-grade teacher tone of voice . . . partly light-hearted, but nonetheless exacting.

"One. I did a little efficiency study for my route last year—took a look at six overall routes in the east part of town. It was very well received. Actually, it resulted in my being assigned the route that took me to your house."

"Good move," said Molly. "So far I'm in favor of efficiency studies in the post office."

"The report got passed up, and about ten months ago, I was asked to do a similar study for three routes in the west part of town. Which I did."

"Glad you didn't get reassigned," Molly said.

"Me, too." *Geez and more geez . . . what if she asks the local postmaster to verify any of this.*

"Well, it got passed up and suddenly, I was called by the big boss guys who wanted to know exactly how I had done what I had done—which had resulted in a significant increase in efficiency and a related significant decrease in man-hours, which also meant a significant decrease in employees . . . ."

"So you are a part of the unemployment picture?" Molly asked.

"Didn't mean to be," said Peter. "Really—I just wanted a personal route with more shade in the summer."

"Aha," said Molly, "personal desires come to the fore."

"Of course!" said Peter. "And the use of a cart."

"Which gives you *four* vehicles," said Molly. "Every guy who has three personal vehicles should certainly have one company car, too."

"Absolutely," Peter said with a laugh. Quick wit and a good memory—combined factors that only added to the reasons why he liked bantering with Molly.

"So," said Peter, "I'm being sent to a couple of other cities to see if my formulas work there, and who knows what after that. I've told them all that I insist on being home by Christmas."

"Christmas!" said Molly. "Let's see. That would be about 342 days from now."

"Give or take a couple."

"I don't think I'm liking this," Molly said.

"I'm not liking the part about being away from you," said Peter. *At least, a bit of the truth.*

"Duly noted!" Molly said, mimicking Peter's early use of the phrase. "But that brings us to issue number two."

"You have a mind like a bulldog," Peter said, adding quickly, "And I mean that in a good way— you don't let go until you get an answer to a question."

"Right," said Molly. "I'll let that slide for now. But tell me, if you are the head of this project, why can't you headquarter that project right here in River City, so to speak."

"Like I said, I have to go to a couple of places to do on-the-ground research. And then I've got to work with a small team of computer types that are being assembled. Who knows . . . I may be able to convince them that we need to locate the entire project in that vacant office building about a half mile from your house!"

"I do not have a clue about any vacant office building," Molly said, "but I'll take your word on it . . . and second the motion for relocation."

"There's some good news," said Peter.

"And it is?"

"I think the United States Postal Service is going to give me at least one long weekend a month so I can fly home."

"How long is a long weekend?"

"Four days—Thursday night through Monday night."

"Consider them booked," Molly said. And then realizing that she probably was taking some things for granted far more than she had a right to, added, "But only if you want to have them booked."

"I do," Peter said.

"And in the meantime, will you call me sometimes?"

"Probably more than you want to be called," Peter said.

"Not possible," Molly said.

"I'm glad."

14

The next Saturday morning, Molly had a strong urge to lace on her walking shoes when she awoke at six o'clock. "Let's go exploring," she said aloud, and when Houndcat opened his eyes to see if there as anybody else in the room she added, "Just kidding. I won't require you to go along."

The day was clear. The temperature was brisk, but with no wind, and a long walk seemed like a splendid idea. Molly headed west.

A turn or two later, she found herself in the cul-de-sac that ended with what she had dubbed "The Christmas Deco House."

A neighbor—directly across the cul-de-sac emerged just as Molly made her U-turn. Seeing the neighbor also in walking shoes she said, "Hey, are you out for a walk, too?"

"I am!" the neighbor said brightly. "Mind if I join you?"

"I'd enjoy the company," Molly said. "I don't know very many of my neighbors. And I haven't been a regular at exercise outside the gym. Hope I can keep up."

"I doubt if that will be a problem," the neighbor replied. "I'm starting in again. New Year's resolution, you know. I'm likely to be the one who can't keep up."

"We'll just have to be gentle with each other," Molly said. "My name is Molly."

"I'm El," the neighbor said. "Short for Ellen."

"Have you lived in the neighborhood long?" Molly asked.

"About four years," said El. "And you?"

"About the same. I live a couple of streets over."

"Truth be told," El said, "I probably wouldn't have recognized you if you lived just two doors down. I don't think I've been the best of neighbor. Maybe that will kick in this year. In the past, I used to walk pretty regularly, but I was usually out here on the streets as the sun was coming up. Not many people in our neighborhood walk at that time."

"Saturday morning is a good time to start at nine o'clock, I think," said Molly. "The joy of sleeping in and the pain of exercise both experienced well before brunch."

"I like that approach," the neighbor replied.

El then added, "I stopped the dawn thing when it suddenly no longer seemed like the safest time to be roaming about outside."

"Did something happen?" Molly asked. It was difficult for her to imagine anything dangerous happening at *dawn* in her neighborhood—or frankly, at any time of day or evening.

"Not directly," said El. "It was just a feeling I had."

"But something must have prompted that feeling."

"Have you ever walked my street much?" El asked.

"No."

"Then you may not have noticed that the house directly across from me in the cul-de-sac still has its Christmas decorations up."

"Oh?" Molly said. "Some people do have a little trouble taking them down before January is in full swing."

"January," said El with a little harrumph to her word. "That would be entirely acceptable. I'm talking NEVER taken down."

"Really," said Molly, not wanting to give any clues about what she already knew. "Never?"

"Never, ever. Up all year."

"That's kinda strange," said Molly.

"I think so," said El. "My husband thinks its none of my business and he also doesn't think its strange—in fact, he thinks that it probably would save him a couple dozen hours a year if he never had to put up or take down Christmas decorations—inside the house or outside."

"Ah, the efficiency of men," said Molly. *Would Peter agree? He might!* "For the record, I think it's strange."

"Glad to hear it!" said El.

"How does that relate to your decision to stop walking at dawn?"

"Well . . . where to start," El said with hesitation. "In the first place, I don't think anybody actually lives at that house. I think it being used for a business. The people who live next door to the house think so, too."

"Do you know what kind of business?"

"No," said El. "And that's part of what's weird about it all. A blue car shows up about 8:45 Monday through Friday, pulls into the garage, and then pulls out of the garage about 4:45 every afternoon. Like clockwork. The car has one person in it. It might be a woman, but the neighbor next door—her name is Ginny—thinks it might *not* be a woman. If it is a woman, she has a very bad wig and very gaudy sunglasses. It doesn't make sense to either one of us why a woman would wear sunglasses on rainy days, but the driver of this car does. And it doesn't make sense to us why a *woman* would leave up Christmas decorations all year. It just seems weird. Both Ginny and I think the person running a business out of this house is a man dressed up to look like a woman."

"But why do that? Why not just be a man who comes and goes . . . ."

"Exactly."

"Anyway . . . given all that, it was definitely something new and different when the car pulled into the neighborhood one morning at dawn, just as I was getting ready to walk out my front door. I closed the door—I don't think anybody in the car saw me do that—and looked through the curtains. Three men got out of the car. Two of them were big guys—really big guys. They opened the trunk of the car and pulled out several large boxes, and another box or two from the backseat. Then a small van showed up and the guys pulled several big boxes out of it."

"What did they do with the boxes?"

"Stacked them along the sides of the garage, which was lined with boxes of all shapes and sizes. At first I thought maybe the boxes were empty, but it took two of them to carry some of the boxes. Then the van drove away. Then the car drove away."

"They just unloaded boxes?"

"Yes. But they kept looking around as if they were trying to see if anybody was watching them. They did their work very quickly. They were only there unloading for five minutes, maybe less."

"The business owner didn't stay?"

"No. And the driver of the car did not have the hair and sunglasses we usually see . . . ."

"Then what?" Molly asked, sensing more to the story.

"Then at 8:45 the blue car came back into the neighborhood, with the driver having longish blonde hair and sunglasses—just like always."

"Do you think something funny is going on?"

"You mean like criminal?"

"Yes."

"I don't know. Ginny doesn't know. But we wonder. The UPS truck usually comes once or twice a day, bringing smaller packages and picking up packages that are left on the porch. Nobody ever answers the door when those packages come and go."

"So you have no idea what kind of merchandise is coming and going?"

"Right. What I do know is that I am glad those big guys that came at dawn didn't see me. They gave me the creeps. They looked like the kind of thugs you see on TV crime shows."

"Did you see them just that one time?"

"Just once," said El. "I got up several mornings after that to see if anybody showed up at dawn. Then I decided that maybe I'd just give up walking the neighborhood and go the gym." She then added with a little laugh, "Only trouble was, I never went to the gym. I just quit walking."

Molly asked, "Did you and Ginny ever try to introduce yourselves to the person in the house?"

"We thought about that. We thought about being the kind of neighbors who show up with a cake to say, 'Hey, welcome to the cul-de-sac.'"

"But you didn't do that, did you?"

"No. In the first place, the person who comes and goes from that house was there long before me.

And, quite frankly, both Ginny and I are a little scared to go and let whoever comes and goes from there see our faces and associate us with our respective homes."

"It's that creepy?"

"It is to me," said El. "I mean . . . think about it . . . this person *never* takes down Christmas decorations?"

"What about the yard? Who does the yard work?"

"Well that's another strange thing. We don't really know. There's a kid who runs the lawnmower and edger, but we never see him come and go from the street. He seems to come from the backyard and it takes him all of about ten minutes to do the yard work and he disappears back behind the house."

"Do you think he comes from the neighbor behind that house?"

"That's my guess. But Ginny asked a friend of hers who lives on that street about the people who live in the house behind the "Christmas Store"— that's what I call the house . . . and she told Ginny that an old man lives in that house . . . by himself."

"Let's turn here," Molly suggested. She liked the phrase Christmas Store, but liked her own name for the house even better: Christmas Deco Depot. She decided that would definitely be her nickname for the house.

"Okay," El said when Molly told her what she had decided to nickname the house, and then she said "okay" again when they got to the intersection and Molly turned right.

They walked toward the end of the block, which turned sharply north, and Molly asked as she nodded to one house in particular, "Do you think that is the house directly behind the Christmas Deco Depot?"

"Yes, I think it is," said El, looking carefully at the roofline of the house behind it. "What are you thinking?"

"I'm thinking that two weird neighbors live close to each other," said Molly.

"What does that mean?"

"It means that the house with the old man may also have some weirdness going on. I can't say for sure, and I don't want to spread gossip that might not be true. But let me ask one of my friends a couple of questions and get back to you."

"Wanna walk again?" asked El.

"Yes," said Molly. But I work during the week so I can't walk until later in the day—I usually get home about five, and these days, of course, it's dark by then."

"The dark is okay with me," said El. "As long as I'm not alone."

"I hear you," said Molly. "And you did say that the Christmas Deco Depot person leaves before five o'clock in the afternoon."

"Yes."

"So the coast might be clear."

"Let me write down my phone number so you can call me on Monday. I'll be eager to hear what your friend says about the potential yard-guy's house."

Molly was glad for a walking partner. Glad that she was getting to know a neighbor. And eager to talk to Peter.

15

Peter didn't call on Saturday, but when he called on Sunday evening, Molly was quick to say, "You started something."

"Alright," said Peter, "I'll bite."

"You got me thinking about my neighbors. And you got me walking."

"Then I started not just one, but TWO things!" said Peter jokingly.

"I met the gal that lives opposite the Christmas Deco Depot and we walked the neighborhood together."

"The Christmas what?"

"That's my name for the house that has the omnipresent Christmas decorations. El—short for Ellen—is the woman who lives opposite the house on the cul-de-sac. She was headed out for a walk as I was making a U-turn in the cul-de-sac and we walked together. She calls the house the Christmas Store, but I have decided to call it the Christmas Deco Depot."

"Does El think the house is being used as a business?"

"Yes," said Molly.

"Bingo!" said Peter. "I think I told you that the next-door neighbor of the house also thinks that's the case."

"The next-door neighbor is named Ginny . . . and yes, she also thinks it's a business."

"Do either El or Ginny know what kind of business?"

"No."

"Aha . . . a neighborhood mystery."

"I'm feeling like Nancy Drew."

"Nancy who?" asked Peter.

"Oh . . .I forgot . . . you were probably into the Hardy Boys. Nancy Drew was a teenage mystery solver, very popular when my mother was a girl. There's a whole series of books called Nancy Drew Mysteries. I read the entire shelf of them that my mother had saved and loaned to me when I was about ten or so."

"Alright . . . Nancy Drew . . . mysteries. I take it Nancy Drew solved neighborhood mysteries."

"Mostly."

"Be careful," said Peter tenderly. He suddenly felt very protective. Perhaps the Gray Tudor wasn't the only house in Molly's neighborhood that was problematic.

"I will be," said Molly. His tender tone had caused a small lump to form in her throat. "Actually, *we* will be. I'm not going to do any sleuthing about this without El, and maybe Ginny, too."

"Good."

"It's nice to know you care," said Molly, trying to be a little casual.

"I do care, Molly," said Peter without hesitation. "I care a great deal."

"I'm glad," she said softly. And then, as if almost forgetting, she said, "El said that the person who does the lawn mowing at that house is a teenager who seems to come from the backyard— sorta out of nowhere—and disappears into the backyard when he's done. But they never see him come and go on the street. I think the house directly behind the Christmas Deco Depot is the house where the old guy is growing pot."

"I think you're right," said Peter.

"Do you think some kind of drug thing is going on?" asked Molly.

"Maybe. But that doesn't quite fit. Why all the UPS traffic? I've never known anybody to ship pot by UPS."

"Good point," said Molly. "I think El and I might see if we can talk Ginny into letting us peak over her fence to see if there's a gate of some kind between the Hemp House and the Christmas Deco Depot."

"The Hemp House?" Peter asked, and then immediately laughed. Molly's penchant for nicknames was almost as good as his . . . and Lance's, for that matter. If Ian could by Lyman, and Tabitha could be Tams, and he could be Liam, and Sterilyn could be Bait . . . well, then, Molly most certainly could live in a neighborhood with a Hemp House and a Christmas Deco Depot. She was clever, and that was yet another thing Peter Lorgham liked about Molly . . . immensely so.

"You know," Molly said reflectively, "none of this is really any of my business. Not really. I hope I can remember the difference between curiosity and snoopiness."

"It's a good thing to remember."

16

Molly didn't walk with El for two more days, at which point they also spotted Ginny carrying groceries into her house and they asked her if they might look over her back fence to see if there was a gate between the Christmas Deco Depot and the house behind it.

"Sure," said Ginny. "How about right now?" She pointed to a small stepladder in the garage. "I'll put the groceries away and join you in a couple of minutes."

It only took a few minutes for Molly and El to haul the ladder into the backyard and set it up. And then only a few seconds for Molly to climb the ladder just to the point of being able to see over the fence. Sure enough, the back property line had a hedge that concealed a rather high chain-link fence, and in the corner, she spotted a small gate. It had a chain and lock on it, but at least the mystery was solved about the lawn mowing. The gate was wide enough for a lawn mower.

"I have a hunch that whoever mows the lawn has a key," said El after she, too, had climbed the ladder to have a look. "Did you notice that the back of the house has as many Christmas decorations as the front?"

"Hadn't noticed," Molly said, as she prepared to climb the ladder again for another look.

"Strange," she said as she descended the ladder. "Part of the windows are covered with heavy drapes, and part have no window coverings and plenty of Christmas stuff on full display. Including fake snow on the small paned windows. I didn't know fake snow could last that long."

"Do you think there's anything about all this that we should report?" asked Ginny as she came back outside. "This neighbor is the strangest neighbor I've ever had."

"I don't know what we'd say," said El. "Strange neighbor has an obsession with Christmas decorations. Hardly headline news."

"And hardly a crime," added Molly. "It might be a cover for something . . . but what? And what's to say the thing being covered up is criminal activity?"

"You're right," said El. Ginny nodded in agreement.

"I told a friend about this neighbor," Ginny added. "She asked me if I thought the person had a meth lab in the house. I told her I didn't think so. Who would ship out meth by UPS? And surely if supplies for making meth were being sent to the house on a regular basis, somebody in some pharmacy somewhere might get suspicious."

"It's a puzzlement," said Molly. And then with a laugh, she added, "I like working puzzles. This is just about my level of intrigue!"

Ginny and El nodded in agreement. "Nancy Drew," they said in unison.

"You've read her, too!" said Molly. It was neighborhood bonding at its best.

During their walk, they did little conversing. They were keeping a faster pace than before. The ladder episode had left them scrambling to get a half-hour walk finished before it become fully dark.

As they rounded their last turn to head for home, Molly suddenly spotted a familiar person getting into a car parked to the side of the road in their direct path.

"Mrs. Glossman!" she called. "Is that you?"

Mirabelle Glossman turned from the open door of her car and peered into the dusk of the evening. "Yes?"

"It's Molly Herman. I was at your house at Thanksgiving—with Ian—and then I saw you at the country club for the ball on New Year's Eve, with Peter."

"Oh, yes, dear!" Mrs. Glossman replied, taking in the full array of her walking gear—hat, scarf, gloves, sweats. "I remember you! I just have never seen you in . . . well . . . anything other than holiday clothes. Is this your neighborhood?"

"It is. This is my neighbor and new friend, Ellen."

"Glad to meet you," said El, glad for a breather but trying not to huff and puff too much.

"Likewise," said Mrs. Glossman, who then added, "I have just had the most amazing thing happen."

"Oh?" Molly replied.

"The man who lives in this house is an old friend of mine—Edgar Carvill the second. No 'junior,' mind you—the *second*. We went to elementary school together. And lo and behold, he called me a couple of days ago and told me that he had found my peacock brooch in a beat-up mail packet by his front steps."

"How strange," said Molly.

"Strange, indeed. I came right over, wondering if it really was *my* peacock, and sure enough, it was."

At this, Mrs. Glossman reached into her car and pulled out what appeared to be about half of a thoroughly mangled mailing envelope, and from it, she retrieved what was, without doubt, the most beautiful bejeweled brooch Molly had ever seen.

"Wow," Molly said as Mrs. Glossman handed her the brooch. "This is amazing."

The brooch was about six or seven inches long, definitely a peacock but the plumage of the bird was draped down, almost giving the bird the appearance of a parrot. The brooch was a combination of cloisonné and jewels, with plenty of emphasis on jewels. It was stunning, and heavy.

"It's been my signature piece of jewelry for decades," said Mrs. Glossman. "I always liked the fact that the peacock wasn't portrayed as strutting—just walking about the barnyard, but that it was a peacock nonetheless. Beautiful, but not needing others to admire its glory."

Molly nodded. *A good bit like Mirabelle Glossman, herself.*

"I was just sick when it went missing. I had it when I went to the club for a birthday celebration dinner the week after New Year's. I didn't have it the next day. But, nobody at the club had seen it, and it wasn't in my car—I drove my driver crazy demanding that he look and look and look again. And then Edgar called. How it ended up *here* is a total mystery to me."

Molly nodded again as she handed the brooch back to Mrs. Glossman. "I'm glad you have it back," she said.

"Indeed."

"It's amazing that Mr. Carvill found it," Molly added. "It obviously wasn't delivered to his address. If it had been, we could take it up with Peter!"

"Peter?" And then as if putting some pieces together, she said, "Oh, yes. I heard he had been delivering the mail in this neighborhood. But . . . "

"He's not the mailman right now, though," said Molly.

"No," confirmed Mrs. Glossman. "I'm glad to hear that you know he's not. Does that mean that you are continuing to see this wonderful grandson of mine?"

Molly could feel herself blushing but knew that Mrs. Glossman wouldn't be able to see that in the growing darkness.

"He's a wonderful man. And yes, I think it would be fair to say that we're still seeing each other."

"Good!" said Mrs. Glossman with enthusiasm. "If you promise not to tell him, I'll tell *you* that he's my favorite grandson. Has more sense and more nobility about him than any of the others."

Nobility. Molly smiled at hearing the word used in reference to Peter. She agreed, but couldn't imagine that anybody other than Mrs. Glossman might understand just why that word applied.

"Since you mentioned Peter," Mrs. Glossman continued, "I think I'll save this tattered old mail envelope for him to see. It might give him some ideas about how to improve mail security."

Then, aware that it was fully *dark*, no longer on the side of *dusk*, Mrs. Glossman said, "I need to let you girls be getting on with your walk. It's dinner time!"

Molly and El said their farewells and resumed their walk.

Changing from her walking clothes to evening loungewear, Molly wondered if Peter knew that his Grams was a long-term friend of Mr. Carvill. Her neighborhood was turning out to be more interesting by the day.

17

"I think you need to fly through the ol' home town on your way out to Portland," Lance said.

"Would like nothing better," said Peter. "But why the sudden benevolence."

"Not exactly benevolence. There are a couple of missing info bits in the Chuminksi case. Bait clammed up at a couple of points in her deposition, and the brass thinks she might open up to you if she found herself talking about her relationship with Chuminski in more of a social setting."

"Sterilyn—or Bait, as you call her—hardly considers me a close confidant."

"I thought you told me one time that she had opened up to you about her relationship with your cousin, and that you were surprised at how candid she had been and how astute her observations had been. You told me you thought she was more savvy than she wanted most people to believe she is."

"True, true. I haven't seen her in at least two years, though."

"But it could be arranged, right?"

"It could. My grandmother could probably be cajoled into hosting a little luncheon that I could crash."

"Then do it," said Lance. "Here's what we need to know." He handed Peter a fairly thick file folder and said, "I took the liberty of booking you on the 3:30 flight out on Thursday. You're headed for Portland on Monday. That should give you plenty of time for a casual investigative conversation."

"Can I take this folder with me?"

"Overnight to your hotel, yes. On the plane, no."

"Guess that tells us both what I'll be doing late into the night," said Peter.

"I'm looking out for Molly' best interests."

"No problem there. If I wasn't reading this dossier I'd be asleep, not out on the town. If you *really* had Molly's best interests at heart, it would be good for me to show up well-rested!"

"Sleep on the plane," said Lance dryly.

"And if Bait doesn't open up?"

"I'm betting she will," said Lance.

18

Molly was ecstatic, of course, at the sudden news that Peter was headed her way the next day. "How long can you stay?" she asked.

"Until oh-dark-hundred Monday."

Three days! She would make the most of them.

"When do I get to see you?" she asked, knowing that he would undoubtedly have a ride from the airport. "I'd offer to pick you up, but . . . ."

"Thanks. The plane gets in late. Two stops between thee and me. How about a seven o'clock breakfast Friday morning before your work day starts."

"Perfect," she said. "Shall I meet you somewhere?"

"Sandy's."

"Great. Love their cinnamon rolls."

After Peter hung up, Molly called her boss. "I need to take a personal day Friday. The McCutchen project is ready to roll. The folder is on my desk. I was going to hand it to you in the morning."

"Great. We can go over the gory details tomorrow."

"It's pretty straightforward. The numbers all line up in our favor."

"If I need you, Friday, I can get you on your cell?"

"Absolutely."

"Have a good time," her boss replied. She was glad to have a supervisor on her side.

Peter's second call on Wednesday evening was to Grams.

"Grams, I need your help," he began after the usual pleasantries and the exchange of a bit of family gossip.

"You know I'll do whatever I can," said Grams. "Does it have anything to do with that darling girl Molly?"

"No," Peter said, a little surprised that she had brought up Molly, but also more than a little pleased that he had referred to her as "that darling girl." He continued, "It has to do with my needing to get some official information out of Sterilyn."

"Sterilyn? Now that's a surprise."

"For me, too."

"You did say *official* information?"

"Yes."

"Not much I can think about that girl that warrants the word *official*. Unless you know something about the status of her relationship with Ian that I don't know."

"No, nothing like that," said Peter. "You'll know about any official hook-up between Ian and Sterilyn long before I will. It does have to do with a relationship, however—more specifically, the relationship she had with that Russian guy a year ago. Before she resumed things with Ian."

"I think he was Russian mafia," said Grams. Then, lowering her voice to a whisper, she asked, "Is this a secure line?"

Peter laughed. He was always a little surprised at how "current" his grandmother always seemed to be. And how quick. And how insightful. *I want to be like her when I grow up*, he said to himself.

"As secure as you can get at a chain hotel," he replied, and then added, "I'm calling on my cell but I'm pretty sure there are no surveillance devices in my room."

"Good. No bugs."

"Hey . . . I didn't say no *bugs* . . . but let's not go there."

"Let's not," Grams agreed.

"Unfortunate choice of terminology to describe electronic spy devices," said Peter.

Grams resumed a normal speaking voice as she asked, "Do *you* think he was Russian mafia? That Noam Chimpanzee person."

"I think it was Chuminksi, Grams."

"Whatever. I thought he looked a little like a chimpanzee—visual associations do help the old memory, you know."

"A chimpanzee?"

"Long arms. Lots of facial hair. Back to the question, do you think he was Russian mafia?"

"I'll tell you a whole lot more, Grams, after I have a spontaneous lunch-time conversation with Sterilyn."

"Oh," said Grams. "And when is that happening?"

"Saturday, at your table in the sunny nook off the kitchen."

"I see. And what time is this luncheon?"

"Well, actually, it's a lunch with just you and Sterilyn. You know—you've been meaning to get her opinion on a few things and haven't really had a chance to talk to her much since she came back into Ian's life, and . . . well, that sort of thing."

"I see."

"And then I just happen to pop in unannounced and spontaneously about a half hour into your lunch together, and you offer me food and I can't resist whatever it is that you made . . . ."

"Catered in."

"That, too. You know that I eat whatever you put before me."

"It's a family rule."

"So I sit down. And then you have to leave to answer the phone."

"Are you going to send me a script for all this drama?"

"If there's anybody who doesn't need a script, it's you, Grams!"

"And this is the great help I'm being asked to give to you and for the good of my country?"

"It is."

"When will we talk again about the logistics of what you'd like to eat and who is going to call me on the phone and how long I have to talk to that phone friend, and so forth and so on?"

"Well, I'm having breakfast with Molly early Friday morning and I thought maybe I'd stop by after that."

"I'll be here. I have a tea to attend later that day but I'm looking at my diary right now and it appears that I can be here until a little before three. In the meantime, I'll call Sterilyn and see if she is free for lunch at noon on Saturday. And if she isn't, then what?"

"Tea. Sunday lunch. Sunday tea."

"Good to have options." And then, fearing Peter might be ready to hang up, "And Peter!"

"Yes."

"I like this Molly girl."

"So do I, Grams."

"I saw her a few days ago while she was out for a walk in her neighborhood."

"What were you doing in her neighborhood?"

"I'll tell you about it when I see you Friday."

"No hints?" Peter teased.

Grams teased back, "Not a one. You're not the only one in this family who can be a secret agent."

If you only knew, Peter thought. *If you only knew.*

19

"I haven't known you all that long," said Ellen, "but I'm guessing that there's a story behind that smile on your face."

"Was I smiling?"

"Like the Cheshire cat in Alice in Wonderland."

"The guy I started seeing at the first of the year has been out of town and he's flying in late tonight and I'm seeing him for breakfast first thing in the morning. So, we've got to walk fast so I can sleep fast so tomorrow morning can get here fast."

"That's what I used to tell my parents on Christmas Eve. I have to eat fast so I can take my bath fast so I can get to bed fast so tomorrow morning can get here fast!"

"Speaking of which," said Molly. "Anything new at the Christmas Deco Depot?"

"Nothing observed. Any more information about the mysterious package with the beautiful bauble over on 73rd Street?"

"No, but thanks for reminding me. I must not forget to tell Peter about that in the morning."

"Quite the mysterious little neighborhood we have here," said El. "Who knew?"

"By the way," Molly said. "See that house up ahead on the left? Just up the hill toward the cul-de-sac?"

"Yeah, what about it?"

"Do you know anything about the people who live there?"

"A little," said El. "Well, a little more than little but not a whole lot."

Molly laughed, as El continued, "That house is one of the three houses that is at the back of our lot."

"You have three backyard neighbors?"

"Strange but true. We've got a big v-shaped lot. Well, the 'v' is more like a flat-topped 'v.' Our yard backs up to three different houses. That one with the grey trim is one of them. It's at the top of the 'v' and the yard they have is also a rather flat-topped 'v' in its shape."

"Interesting."

"Why did you ask? El said.

"Just curious," Molly said. "A friend told me to steer clear of the house but didn't say why."

"Funny you should say that," El said.

"Why 'funny'?"

"The house has always given me the creeps. And what little I know about the people who live there gives me pause, too."

"What little do you know?"

"I know that we had a perfectly good wooden privacy fence—a six-foot one—and they built a red brick fence on their side of the property that extends above our fence by a good two feet. They planted a brambly sort of bush that has the ability to grow between our wood fence and their brick fence. Which makes for a very interesting visual in our backyard."

"I guess," said Molly.

"And . . . when they were building the brick fence my husband noticed that they were putting pieces of broken glass at the top of the bricks—not that you can see the top of the fence now, but the glass was put there anyway."

"Well, you don't have to worry about anybody climbing into your backyard from that side," Molly said.

"But why would they be so concerned that somebody might be crawling into *their* backyard?"

"No clue."

"And . . . ."

"There's more?"

"The house has a second floor but we have never seen the curtains pulled open on that floor. The curtains aren't just normal bedroom-style curtains. They are the heavy black-out kind of curtains."

"That's a little odd."

"Especially since those windows would have the most amazing north-and-east light."

"Anything else?" Molly asked.

"They cut down just enough trees to put in a spa. They probably have more trees in the backyard than four other houses combined."

"Do you ever hear the spa running?" Molly asked, not at all sure why that question would come to mind.

"Funny you should ask that," said El. "The answer is yes . . . and no. We never hear it at night. But sometimes in the late afternoon. I looked into the yard one time when I heard the spa—since I've never seen anybody come or go from the front door of the house, although like I said, I didn't walk this neighborhood for quite a while before we started walking together."

"How did you look into the yard with such a high fence?"

"There's a little portion of one brick that wasn't mortared in right. We had a couple of planks of our wooden fence go wonky last summer so we removed them, planning to replace them, and I noticed that brick and in fiddling with it, realized I could actually pull it out of the wall."

"Seriously."

"And just at the time I was holding that pulled-out brick in my hand, I heard the spa start up. It's really a pretty noisy one."

"So you looked through the wall?"

"I did. I put the brick back in sideways so it was only about a half-brick hole, and I became a peeping Tom . . . or a peeping Ellen."

"What did you see?"

"I saw a teenagerish girl get into the spa, tie up her hair, and then a guy came out of the house. He had on dark glasses and was fully dressed—no swim trunks. And he handed the girl a martini glass filled with a drink of some kind. And sat down by the edge of the spa, kicked off his shoes and pulled up his pants legs, and dangled his legs in the water."

"And . . . ."

"And I just kept watching, Molly. Don't know why. I was just stuck there somehow. Glued to the hole in the brick fence."

"For how long?"

"Oh, five minutes or so. I think I was expecting that maybe this chick would pull him into the water, or I don't know. . . .Anyway, she suddenly went limp and dropped the martini glass into the water, and he grabbed her by the knot of hair she had created and pulled her up and then put both hands under her armpits and pulled her out of the spa. She was as limp as a dishrag."

"You're kidding. He spiked her drink? Is that what you're saying?"

"It sure looked that way."

"Then what happened?"

"She was lying by the side of the spa and he looked around. I was plenty scared he'd see the hole in the fence and I moved the brick at an angle. When I peeked back through an even narrower slit, I saw him carrying her into the house, sorta plopped over his shoulder like a sack of something."

"And she was still limp?"

"Oh, yes. Her eyes were closed. Her head was bobbing. She was out cold."

"What did you do?"

"I decided I'd seen far more than I ever should have seen. I put the brick back into the hole so that it appeared as it had before."

"Was that the only time you took a look into the backyard?"

"No."

"No?"

"My curiosity got the better of me a few days later when I went out to change the sprinklers and heard the spa go on. I moved the brick just enough to peek through the fence."

"What did you see this time?"

"The same thing I saw the first time! Except that this time the girl had dark hair—the first girl was blonde. Similar drink. Same scenario."

"This guy is doping girls for sex!" Molly exclaimed.

"Don't know about the sex," Ellen said. "But the doping sounds right—maybe. No proof. Just what I *think* I saw."

"Did you tell anybody?" Molly asked.

"No. You are the first person I've ever told," Ellen said. "My husband doesn't even know about it."

"Why didn't you tell him?"

"He'd tell me I had no business looking through the fence and that it was none of my concern. And besides, it only happened twice in a space of about ten days, and it was last summer . . . and my husband got fence planks the next weekend and repaired our side of the fence, so that was that."

"Wow," said Molly.

"Yeah, wow," said Ellen.

They looked at each other and as if on cue, they erupted in laughter. There was nothing funny—not really—about what Ellen had seen or said. There was nothing funny about what might be going on in the house with the grey trim. But there they stood, two neighbors who were new friends feeling as if they were living in a neighborhood filled with intrigue and mystery. And both of them were totally unlike any detectives they had ever seen on television and totally inept in their spy skills . . . and they knew it. It was just too funny for words. So they laughed.

"Quite the little neighborhood we have here," Molly finally said.

"More than we ever knew from the realtors before we moved in!" Ellen added.

"And I think I've just about overdosed on endorphins."

"It sure made the walk go faster, though, right?" asked Ellen.

"Absolutely. And now for a fast jog home and a fast dinner and a . . . ." Molly's voice trailed off as she turned and headed for home.

20

Peter was at Sandy's at 6:30. He was just that excited to see Molly. He didn't want to miss a minute. She, feeling the same way, showed up at 6:35.

"We're a couple of early birds," she said as she entered the café and saw him already occupying a booth toward the back.

He kissed her lightly and said, "but no worms, alright?"

She smiled at his quick wittedness. "Only cinnamon rolls, and perhaps their cheesy egg casserole."

"My favorites, too," said Peter. And for the next hour, they jabbered at each other nonstop."

"You'd think we haven't talked in months," said Peter.

"Am I delving too deep into details?" Molly asked.

"No deeper than I am. I like details."

"Lots of guys don't."

"I'm not lots of guys," Peter said with a grin.

"No, indeedy," Molly replied.

"And I intend to keep it that way."

Molly blushed, but then, who wouldn't have?

"And I haven't even told you all that is going on in the neighborhood," Molly said, changing direction for the conversation. Sandy's was not exactly the place for romantic confessions—not that there was anything wrong with Sandy's, but old black-and-white tiles on the floor, black leather booths, bright lights, and artificial red geraniums and red-and-white check café curtains at the windows made for a good breakfast conversation, not a romantic interlude.

"Like what?" Peter asked.

She told him about looking over Ginny's fence, and seeing a chain link fence, and beyond it, the Hemp House. And then about seeing his grandmother and the peacock brooch.

"Really?" Peter said. "I had no idea Grams knew ol' Carvill. But they would be about the same age. I'll have to ask her about that."

"I was surprised that he recognized the brooch as belonging to her," said Molly, "but then again, she did say that it was her 'signature piece.'"

"It is," Peter said. "Anybody who is around Grams more than one or two times is likely to have seen her wearing that pin. In the first place, it's huge. Hard to miss. Way beyond discreet. And it's loaded with all kinds of carats—carats of diamonds, carats of rubies, carats of emeralds, carats of sapphires. All of them *real* stones, no fakes. I've warned her for years that Mr. Peacock is an invitation to be mugged."

"The thought crossed my mind, too," said Molly.

"She laughs and says, what makes you think it is MISTER Peacock."

"'Aren't they the ones with the stunning feathers?' I ask. And she says, 'Maybe in real life. I don't know. But this is not a real peacock so this peacock can be a female peacock if I want it to be.' And I say, 'And do you want it to be a female peacock?' And she says, 'Most definitely.' So I say, 'So MISS peacock is an invitation to be mugged.'"

Peter paused to take a sip of the hot chocolate that the waitress delivered to their table.

"Best hot chocolate in a radius of five hundred miles," he commented.

Molly nodded agreement as she cradled her large mug of hot chocolate.

"And she says . . . " Molly said, releasing the pause button on the conversation under way.

"She says, 'Nobody would mug me for this pin, Peter. In the first place, people who know me and see me wearing it at the club or at a party know that the pin could never be pawned or sold. It's my *signature*.' And then she says, 'And, people who don't know me—the waiters and all—would never guess that the stones are real. They all think its just a gaudy piece of costume jewelry worn by an eccentric old lady who thinks she's pulling a fast one on society, pretending to be rich and glamorous.'"

"Well, that's one way of looking at it," Molly said.

"Grams also has made a point on at least a dozen occasions when we've had this conversation—which is almost as set as a language-lesson dialog between us after all these years—of showing me the triple-fastener on the back of the pin. There are three places where the brooch is bradded to the fastening rod with strange little clip-and-secure devices—European probably—and then there's a chain linking those fasteners. It's about as secure as a brooch can be once it's properly attached and fastened to a garment."

"But apparently it wasn't fastened properly at least once . . . and that, not long ago."

"So . . . I shall have to ask her about this," Peter said. "I'm headed over there later today." After a bit of egg casserole, he added, "Anything else going on in the old neighborhood?"

"Yes," said Molly, back on task. "I saw a guy in the yard of Helene's house and he looked as if he could be about the right age to be one of her sons, so I asked him about his mother. He said that she had been moved to an extended-care facility—the one you recommended. He and his brother hadn't decided what they were going to do about the house. His mother wasn't ready to sell it, but they were pretty sure she'd never be able to live there alone again."

"Hmm," said Peter. "I'm glad they cared enough to come and that they made a good decision . . . at least a good decision in my opinion."

"And," said Molly, "an update on the Hemp House."

"Oh?"

"When Ellen and I looked over the fence, I saw the hedge . . . sure enough, hemp. Very big. And I also saw his greenhouse. I think there are hemp plants growing in there in several sizes?"

"You could tell what the plants were . . . for sure?"

"I went home and looked up the item in question," said Molly, glancing around to make sure nobody at the adjacent booth was paying attention to her. "I think you had the right diagnosis. There were some orchids, too, I think. And lots and lots of African violets in small pots."

"Decoys," said Peter with an impish grin. He didn't really want Molly to think that he was concerned. As a fed, he knew, of course, that Mr. Epstein was flirting with a federal offense. He liked Mr. Epstein, and couldn't help wondering if there wasn't a way out of this apart from turning him in.

A bite of cinnamon roll later, Peter asked, "Anything else?"

For some reason, Molly found herself hesitating when it came to telling Peter about the brick fence and the spa and what Ellen had seen. *Later,* she thought. *I don't need to have him upset with me about any activities related to that house after he told me so forcefully not to have anything to do with the house or its occupants. Not on our first time together and a long weekend ahead.* Still, she knew she would tell him before he flew away on Monday.

"Is it about time for you to go to work?" Peter asked, looking at his watch. "It's almost ten o'clock, Molly! You're late!"

"I took a personal day," Molly said casually.

"Really?"

"Yes. I didn't want to have to hurry through breakfast."

"Does that mean you're mine all day?"

Molly was pleased . . . actually, more than pleased. "If you want me to be yours all day."

"I do!" Peter said. "This is the best news I've heard all day!"

"It's only ten o'clock," said Molly. "And hey . . . is that a comment on my very excellent reporting on the neighborhood."

"Some of your reporting, my dear, just might fall into the class of 'bad news,' don't you think?" said Peter, teasing as he stood to help her out of the booth and into her coat. "I'm glad to know *everything*—good and bad. But here's the deal. I need to see Grams this morning. I'd love for you to go with me. What do you say I follow you to your house and then you go with me to the Mansion? We can play it by ear after that."

"Works for me."

"And, I should warn you upfront. I need to have about a half hour's conversation with Gram in private. Is that okay with you?"

"I'll bring a book," Molly said.

21

Peter was glad that Lance had given him ample hours to digest Sterilyn's deposition and the full dossier of the case, and to formulate at least the beginnings of an approach to take with Sterilyn. He had pretty much decided during the flight what he would say to Grams.

Grams was delighted to see Molly, as he knew she would be. Grams offered her coffee, which Molly declined, and was agreeable when Molly offered to go into another room to read while she and Peter discussed whatever it was that Peter needed to discuss. Grams showed her to the sunroom, a room that was actually already familiar to Molly.

"I really *like* her, Peter," Grams said as she took Peter's arm and guided him into the library and closed the door behind them.

"I know you do, Grams," Peter said. "I like her too."

"No," said Grams. "You aren't hearing me. I *REALLY* like her."

"Yes, Grams. I *REALLY* like her, too. It's serious," Peter said. "At least on my part."

"Good," said Grams. "Now what's all this about Sterilyn?"

"I can't tell you everything," Peter began, "but I can tell you some things."

"You know I never break a confidence," Grams said.

"I do know that," said Peter. "That's why I can tell you *some* things."

"This has to do with your real job, right?" said Grams. "Not the phone-baloney mailman thing."

"Right."

"By the way, does Molly know what you really do?"

"No."

"I see . . . just needed to know, so I'd know where the edge of the cliff is."

"Molly thinks I'm a mailman who has been tapped by the Postmaster General to do a major efficiency study for the post office."

"They need one."

"Maybe. But that's not what I'm really doing . . . so don't get your hopes up."

"So what's with Sterilyn? Why am I having lunch with her tomorrow."

"Is it a go?"

"Yes. She seemed genuinely pleased to be invited. Twelve-thirty. She had a manicure appointment at eleven. What do you want to eat?"

"Well, knowing that it has to be female food . . . ."

"I was thinking some kind of pasta dish—maybe with chicken and Cajun spices, and a salad. That way, you can have a big man portion while Sterilyn and I limit ourselves to small lady-like portions."

"Sounds great."

"Will Molly come, too?"

"No, not at this meeting."

"But soon?"

"Sure."

"Back to the subject at hand. What's with Sterilyn?"

"Well, the foreign guy she was dating— Noam Chuminsky—was probably in her life solely because she comes from big money."

"No surprise there."

"Well, she does have lots of assets," Peter said with a grin.

"I'm not disagreeing. She's got looks and a good figure—although her skin probably isn't going to hold up very well through the years . . . she's got money, she's short on pizzazz and creativity, but she's got manners and she's pretty transparent, and oh, did I mention, she has money."

Peter smiled. Pure Grams at her descriptive best.

"So what did he take her for?" Grams asked.

"As it turns out, Chuminsky probably didn't want Sterilyn's cash as much as he wanted her banks."

"Now there's an interesting twist."

"And more specifically, he wanted information *about* her banks, especially international information."

"So he was Russian mafia," Grams said.

"No, he was more on the espionage side."

"A Russian spy?" Grams said, reducing her voice to a whisper and adding a little whistle of her own—feminine, but a whistle nonetheless.

"He put on his dumb hat with Sterilyn, of course," said Peter. "Told her he was a Russian businessman who was hoping to set up a business to benefit both Russia and America—good foreign relations and world peace and all that."

"Noble," said Grams.

"Not so noble. He told her he didn't really understand American business—capitalism, that is.

Only he always called it capitalonialism to her. He told her that he had grown up with the communist system and he was ignorant when it came to American banking and financing."

"And Sterilyn bought all that. Why not?" said Grams. "Enough truth in all that to sound legitimate."

"Exactly."

"So what was wrong with that?"

"Nothing, at the beginning. Sterilyn apparently was relieved that he wasn't asking her for money. Nor was he asking her to bankroll an international business. She was willing to help him as much as she could as long as she didn't have to fork over any of her own wealth."

"Never said the girl was stupid," said Grams. "So what did she do that was so wrong?"

"Nothing that was actually illegal," said Peter. "What she did was show Chuminsky her financial records—statements, accountant's reports, stock-broker reports, and on and on. She set him up with some of her advisors and her senior bankers in New York. They, in turn, pretty much told him most of their secrets related to decision-making, investing, and in the end, for the right fee, a couple of them told him stuff that truly amounts to insider trading, how to set up offshore accounts so they would *look* legal, and how to launder money."

"Aha. Money laundering. That's when it turned illegal?"

"Among other charges."

"So is Sterilyn in trouble?"

"No. She cut a deal with Justice that she would be absolved of any wrongdoing if she'd tell them exactly who did what, when, and where, and for how much."

"So what is it that you need to find out?" Grams asked.

"Sterilyn neglected to tell them—in her long litany about dates and meetings and weekends with Chuminsky—that they had traveled to Zurich together. Nor did she tell them that she had been to the Grand Caymans with him. When they asked her about those trips on *his* litany of encounters revealed under oath, she just shrugged and said, 'It was all personal.'"

"And the officials don't buy that?"

"No. It was apparently on those trips that certain accounts were opened and funded. Chuminsky accounts. Possible Sterilyn accounts. Perhaps other accounts that link the New York financial types with Russian mafia types and in general, with Russian spy types."

"So what are you supposed to find out?"

"How to set up untraceable off-shore, out-of-the-country accounts."

"Will you tell me how to do it once you find out?" Grams asked with the faintest of grins.

"Of course. We'll both get in on the action," Peter replied, also grinning.

"This all sounds more C.I.A. than F.B.I.," Grams noted.

"With certainty, money was flowing across state lines, as well as out of the country. My partner on another project is C.I.A. and I'm doing him a little bit of a favor, also serving my own yuppy-yups."

"Alright," said Grams. "I'm good to go. Who's going to call me?"

"I'm going to ask Molly to make a call to you. You and Molly are going to plan my surprise birthday party at the club. It could take a while to get all those details down. I need at least twenty minutes with Sterilyn."

Grams stood up. "I feel fully rehearsed."

Peter stood up and agreed, "I believe you will give an award-winning performance."

"Let's get back to Molly."

Molly looked up from her book to see both Peter and Grams grinning. "What gives?" she said.

They told her of the phone call they wanted her to make the next afternoon and she was more than willing to comply. "Is your birthday really on the horizon?"

"It is."

"And could you really be here for a party?"

"I could. In fact, I'm counting on it."

Molly looked at Grams. "And we really get to plan something over the top?"

"Way over the top," Grams replied. "Assuming that means spectacular."

Molly shifted gears. "Did you mention to your grandmother what I told you about her peacock brooch?"

"What's with that?" Peter said, turning to Grams. "Molly says you lost your brooch and that Mr. Carvill found it?"

"Let me go get the mailing envelope," Grams offered. While she was out of the room, Molly said, "I can hardly wait to talk to your grandmother tomorrow."

"I think she'd like for you to call her Grams, and I'm hoping you'll start referring to her as Grams," Peter said. "There are moments when I'm not sure who you are talking about when you say 'your grandmother' or 'Mrs. Glossman.'"

"Grams seems pretty . . . well, family," Molly said. But then, with a flirtatious smile she added, "I'll ask her about it tomorrow."

"Ask her what?" Peter said.

"If I can call her Grams."

"Oh. I thought maybe you were going to ask her about being family?"

"Heavens, no," said Molly. "I barely know you, Peter Lorgham!"

Grams reentered the sunroom and thrust the tattered envelope into Peter's outstretched hands, and then plopped down into an over-stuffed down-filled loveseat filled with overstuffed down pillows. Molly noticed that the design of the fabric was "peacock." She smiled.

"So tell me first about Carvill," Peter said. "I didn't know you knew him."

"I've known him since we were eight years old. His family lived on a ranch outside the city and they moved into town when we were in third grade. He was in every class I had until we graduated from high school. He wore a hand-tied bow tie every day. Nobody else did, mind you, but Ed Carvill the second wasn't just another boy.

"He was scrawny as a kid, but a very handsome teenager, let me assure you of that. He'd still be a good looker if he'd stay clean shaven. He was in bad need of a shave when I saw him last week. Anyway . . . . Mattie Henseley got it into her noggin to date him—we were fifteen at the time—and she never let go of that notion. She was a real flirt, that girl—not all that pretty, but with a personality that people today would call a mix of charm and spunk. Vivacious was my word. Mattie was my friend and I knew Ed would be a significant rung up the social ladder for her and I was glad about that. I did my best to help her land him . . . and she did.

"He went off to college and she went to some sort of finishing school for a year, and they got married when we were all nineteen. Seems young now, but not in those days. She had a baby within a year, and then another baby the next year, and then a third baby the very next year. And then apparently she woke up and decided the baby-a-year plan wasn't for her.

"Ed bought a boat and began to spend more and more of his off-work time at the lake. He told Mattie that the boat was a good magnet for business contacts, and I really have no doubt about that. I never discussed Mattie's love life with her—we just didn't talk about things like that back then, not even with best friends. Mattie seemed happy to have the house to herself and her two boys and one girl. Ed seemed happy at the lake. Eventually he bought a house up there and there were a few times each year when Mattie and the children went to the lake for a week or so. But overall, Mattie lived in the city, and Ed lived at the lake and hosted clients up there, all to great financial advantage. A lot of money can be made in a recreational setting. Ed proved it."

"You wouldn't know it from his current house in town," Peter said.

"That was a gift from Mattie and Ed to their second son. Each child got a house. And a car. Mattie once told me she and Ed felt that they had done their duty as parents once a house and car were signed over. Son number two traded up and Ed bought up the house behind him."

"What happened to Mattie?" Molly asked, and then quickly added, "if it isn't too forward for me to ask?"

"Mattie surprised us all. Ed, most of all," said Grams. "One day she up and announced that she wasn't going to let any more of her life pass her by. The kids were grown, had cars of their own and houses of their own, and she was moving on.

"We really had no idea what she was talking about—she announced all this one day after bridge club. We used to meet once a month for lunch and cards, you know. Anyway . . . we learned that 'moving on' meant moving out of town—way out of town. She had met a Frenchman at a party and she openly admitted to having started an affair with him, and now she was going to move to Venezuela to be with him. We were stunned. We didn't know anybody who had a French lover. And it was almost unthinkable that Mattie Henseley would be brave enough to take such a lover, much less move all the way to South America to be with him.

"When we asked her if she was divorcing Ed she said, 'No, not unless he insists on it. Why would I want to do that? I might want to come home some day?' Said it just like that—as if Ed would be waiting with open arms. Well, actually, he might have, if she had. But Mattie never did come back. We heard about five years ago that she had died."

"In Venezuela?" Molly asked.

"No, actually, in Spain," Gram said. "Apparently she met a Spaniard from Barcelona in Venezuela and she 'moved on' once again. Sure wasn't the Mattie we knew at fifteen, I guarantee you that. She never divorced Ed, and of course, Ed—for his part—never showed any desire to remarry. I think he was a little grateful he never really had to support Mattie once she left for South America. He lived a pretty frugal life and became one of the wealthiest men in town, although you'd never know it."

"Really!" said Peter. "He sure fooled me."

"Like I said, he lived a low-profile life here. All the high living was out at the lake, but even then, from what I've heard, the men who went out there to make business deals with him liked the 'roughing' aspect of his log mansion and fishing for dinner and all that."

"I thought he told me one time that he had a car dealership."

"Oh, that was just a hobby," Grams said. "From the time we all had driver's licenses, Ed always had the best car of anybody in our social set. And, he had a new car every year, sometimes every six months. If it was fast and flash, Ed had to have it. Which totally belied his personality and all of the other low-key aspects of his life as the years went by."

"He told me he lives on a houseboat now," Peter said.

"I'd like to see that houseboat," Grams said. "Are you sure he didn't say yacht?"

"Very sure," said Peter. "The word 'yacht' would have caught my attention."

"Why do you think somebody would have mailed your peacock brooch to Mr. Carvill?" Molly asked.

"I don't think they did," said Grams.

"But Molly said it was at his house, right?" Peter asked, looking first at Grams and then at Molly.

"Ed found what you've got there in your hand in the flower bed by the front steps. He said he almost didn't see it. And I could understand that. He really doesn't have much of a gardener from what I could tell—everything all growing this way and that.

"When he picked up the envelope, Miss Peacock fell out onto the ground under a bush, and when he picked her up, he knew immediately that it was *my* peacock. No question there. He's only seen it a thousand times, at least, since my grandmother first gave it to me."

"So he called and you went and here it is, safely home," said Peter. "But tell me . . . how did you lose it Grams? It's got enough clasps on it to qualify it as the Fort Knox of brooches."

"That's the mystery part. I do not know when or where . . . or how . . . I lost it. I wore it to a party in honor of the Keelers' anniversary—62 and holding, or so Ned Keeler announced with great joy—and the next day, it was nowhere to be found."

"Did you check your coat at the club?"

"No, I kept it with me. The dining room was cold. Or maybe I was just feeling a chill. But, I didn't have it pinned to my coat. I had pinned it to a cashmere shawl. I put that on back of my chair in the dining room with my coat. I'm certain of it."

"Do you have any idea why the person who found it would have returned it to Carvill?" Peter asked.

"That's the real mystery, isn't it?" said Grams. "No clue. He hasn't been to the club for years, as far as I know. Those of us who know him from the foundation of the earth can't recall the last time we saw him out and about *anywhere* in the city. Why somebody would mail Miss Peacock to him is a huge mystery."

Oh, why not, thought Molly. *One more mystery in the neighborhood won't hurt!*

"Ed said he thought a dog must have mauled the envelope. He said a big dog had been roaming the neighborhood lately—dragging its leash as if it had escaped its owner—and he thought he saw it munching on some paper before it ran off after he tried to approach it to see what exactly was in its mouth."

"That would be Tobiah," said Peter. Molly and Grams registered raised eyebrows. "Husky that lives on 79th," Peter added. "We're on a first-name basis, Tobe and me."

Peter looked closely at the envelope.

"Mind if I take this?" he asked.

"No," Grams said. "Maybe the Post Office can figure out a way to spray the mail so dogs naturally want to shy away from it."

"I'm up to my ears in efficiency studies, Grams," Peter said. "I'll see if they can assign me to work on pet and pest deterrents next year."

"And we can all hope that such a study can be conducted from right here!" Molly said. Turning to Grams, she added, "I miss him when he's gone."

"So do I, dear," said Grams.

22

Friday afternoon and evening turned out to be a string of one fun hour after the next. They shopped the mall—Peter needed a new pair of jeans and a new pair of jogging shoes. They went grocery shopping and picked up a video. They stopped by the dry cleaners and bank—pick-up from the former, deposit to the later. And then, Peter asked Molly if she wanted to go to his place to fix dinner, "You've never been to my man cave, have you?" he asked, knowing the answer already.

She was eager to see how Peter lived.

It turned out his "cave" was the top floor of an old brick office building downtown. "The top four floors were turned into condo lofts about six or seven years ago," Peter said. "There were four large lofts per floor. I gutted the top floor and turned the four units into one large space, which I have just about finished out. It's still a bit of a work in progress."

Molly was impressed. The outer walls of the condo were old brick, the ceilings were very high, and the open pipes and ductwork, along with the ceiling, had been painted black and seemed to disappear. She had been expecting that Peter might have a mix of black leather, chrome, and glass as his décor of choice, but was surprised to see that his preference was much more Old English Library— antique wooden furniture, dark green and dark red painted panels strategically placed, lots of books on dark mahogany bookshelves.

"And what's with the telescope?" she said as she went over to the windows overlooking the city skyline.

"All the better to spy out what's happening in town," Peter laughed. "Actually, I've been trying to teach myself a little astronomy. Never hurts to keep learning, you know."

Molly smiled. "I'm taking a class in Italian," she said.

"Italian?"

"Sure, why not?" Molly replied. "You never can tell when somebody might ask you to go to Florence."

Peter opened the door out onto the balcony. "The place didn't originally have a balcony. I had to cut into the wall and create a balcony from what had been indoor space, but I've always been fond of balconies, so I did what I could. It helps me think I have a 'yard.' I pull some of my indoor potted plants out there in the summer."

"You must have somebody watering your plants?"

"Eula. Comes once a week to clean the place, water plants, do laundry. She used to help my mother—I don't like to think how old she is or when she might think she's too old to do a little housekeeping. The work at my place is minimal, I think. And I know she needs the money."

Molly relaxed. The thought of another woman in Peter's cave was not a pleasant thought—but if the woman was old enough to be his grandmother, hey—he was lucky to have found good help.

To Molly surprise, the room beyond the spacious kitchen and eating area was even more like a library than the living area. It had a large fireplace and a big-screen television screen. "This is amazing. A fireplace on what . . . did I see you key into an elevator button above eleven?"

"Right, twelfth floor. But that's if you don't count the mezzanine," he said and then he added teasingly, "It's really the thirteenth floor but I wouldn't want you to get nervous."

Molly smiled. "I'm not superstitious. It feels way higher than that, though."

"It is. The bottom floor is two-stories in one. And then there's the parking garage above the mezzanine. We left the car at the main entrance, but there are also six floors of parking—the entry to the parking garage is on the next street over. The entire building is cut into a hillside so people who pull into the parking garage have little indication they are really entering the third floor of the building."

"So that makes it . . . ."

"Twenty-first floor by normal people's standards."

With that Peter picked up a remote-control device and activated the fireplace, adjusting it down from a roar to a moderate "cozy" fireplace look, complete with sparkling embers.

"Very realistic," Molly said.

"Very convenient," Peter replied. "There's a wood burner in the master bedroom. It has the chimney for that. The space I chose for my bedroom was originally my great-grandfather's office and he burned coal in the corner of his corner office. I must confess, I use this fireplace a lot more than that one."

"You've done an impressive job, Peter," Molly said with sincerity. "Frankly, I can't think of anything about you that doesn't seem to turn out to be impressive."

"And you know one of the things I like best about you, Molly?" Peter said, in her same vein of serious compliment.

"What?"

"A compliment from you means something. I never have the feeling you are blowing sweet nothings into my ears."

"Do you like living downtown?" Molly asked, suddenly feeling a little bashful.

"Very much, actually. I like not having to do yard work. Raking leaves was never my great love. And for that matter, I don't get any thrills from having to hire and supervise people who do enjoy raking leaves."

"It seems very quiet for a Friday night. Is that the altitude or the brick, or is it just that way?"

"It's amazing how quiet the neighborhood is after six o'clock. I can walk to good restaurants and to the concert hall if I want. Groceries aren't readily available, but that's not a big problem. I just stop somewhere on my way home if I need to. I looked into putting in a grocery store a couple of years ago, but the feasibility study didn't show a profit for several years, if then."

"You were going to own a grocery store?" Molly asked as she joined him in chopping up vegetables at the kitchen sink.

"No, I was going to look for a franchise to lease out the space at the back of the first floor. I eventually leased it out as offices."

The light came on. Molly asked somewhat tentatively, "Do you *own* this building?"

"Well, if you mean, am I paying the mortgage on it every month, the answer is 'yes.' So far, it's been a great investment. The trick is to keep the space occupied. And right now, we're at about ninety percent."

"I'm impressed."

"That I own an old brick building that my great-grandfather first built and forgot to leave to me as an inheritance?"

"Impressed that you have ninety percent occupancy."

"It was a real marketing challenge. Good firm, though, took on that challenge and gave the building a name and a look and occupants started signing up. The name of that residential real estate marketing firm is McConnell, Martin, and O'Dell."

"That's where I work," Molly said.

Peter looked at her with a grin. "I know."

"You know?"

"Sure. I saw your name on the roster of employees a few months ago. And I called you at work last week but you weren't there and I didn't leave a message. It was confirmation that you *still* worked at M. M. and O."

"You are very . . . investigative, Peter Lorgham," she said.

"That I am!" he said. *If you only KNEW,* he thought. "If I had known then what I know now, I would have asked you to head up the marketing effort on Downtown One."

"As it turns out, I did help with it. I ran the retail profile study."

"Well . . . then you know all about the grocery idea and the retail space on the first floor."

"Not really. I ran the retail profile *prior* to the building being purchased."

"I'm going to throw together a salad while the sauce is cooking," Peter said. "If you'd like to look around the rest of the floor, be my guest."

Molly took him up on is offer to give herself a self-guided tour. Each finished-out space was spectacular, the views were stunning. She found an additional balcony, and when she came to what was undoubtedly the master bedroom, she had a sudden urge to jump on the bed. She refrained. It was the first time she had thought about how the evening might end. *Why am I always one step behind on seeing where something MIGHT go?* she chided herself.

But, she need not have worried or even felt anxious. She and Peter laughed their way through dinner, watched one video, made bananas Foster and then watched the second video they had picked up, and a little after midnight, Peter offered to take her home since they had a big day ahead on Saturday. "As much as I'd like to sit on this sofa for another two hours just staring into your eyes and kissing you until your lips got sore, I don't think we should."

"I appreciate that," said Molly.

"It isn't that I don't WANT serious physical intensity with you," Peter said, trying to sound as erudite as he was sounding. "It's that I'm not sure I'd want to stop at the appropriate place once we got something started . . . ."

"And you wouldn't trust me to say 'stop'?" Molly asked.

"Oh, I'd trust you with that. Certainly. I just don't want you to *have* to say 'stop.'"

With that, he kissed her passionately—not once, but several times, thoroughly smudging her lipstick and ruffling her hair. She finally pulled away and said with feigned breathlessless, "Why, Mister Lorgham, did thou not hear anything that thou hast just sayeth?"

"Yeah," he said with a grin. "But somehow I didn't think you seemed very convinced that I really do *desire* you, Molly Herman."

"I'm glad you do," she said softly. "And I'm glad you are taking me home . . . right about now."

"I'm shocked that I am, actually," Peter said. "Don't tell any of my guy friends."

23

Peter and Molly had decided that given the late night, they'd meet as soon as he left Grams early the next afternoon. Peter said he had several calls to make before he had lunch at what Peter affectionately called the Mansion, so Molly took advantage of the morning to call Tams.

"Is Petie-Eye home this weekend?" Tams asked.

"He is! And Tams, he's so far from Petie-Eye. I'm thinking he just might be Prince Peter of the Ever After."

"Seriously?" Tams said.

"Could be."

"Then I shall never again call him Petie-Eye. Prince Peter has a much more elegant ring to it."

"You said last time we talked that he had been out of town. Did you ever find out what that was all about?"

Molly explained about the efficiency study and that Peter would be spending considerably more time out of town, not sure how long, and that he was home for the weekend only.

"Have you already checked into airfares?" Tams asked.

"Of course," answered Molly without skipping a beat. "Four hundred and thirty-eight dollars if I fly coach and plan in advance."

"Maybe Peter would buy the ticket?" Tams suggested tentatively.

"He might. He's got a lot more money than you'd think, his working as a mailman and all. But let's see how this weekend ends. Things are so good I am almost scared they are too good."

"You can talk to him about anything and everything?"

"Anything and everything."

"You can really be yourself?"

"Totally."

"You like kissing him?"

"Tremendously."

"He isn't pushing you for more than you want to put out?"

"No. And that's an amazing thing to me. I know he's normal and he wants 'the whole package,' as Ian used to say, but he also knows that I have what Ian described as 'a purity streak.'"

"Peter's okay with that?"

"He is."

"I think you need to lose all references to Ian."

"I was pretty surprised to hear myself even mention him," Molly said. "He had a few phrases that were classics, and those were two of them."

"Back to Peter, he's okay with taking things slow?"

"A few phone calls ago he told me that I was the first woman he had ever dated in slow motion. I asked him what that meant. He said that he was purposefully taking things very slow—because he didn't want to crash the relationship by going too fast around a curve. I thought that was a fun metaphor. I told him I appreciated the slowness. I told him that it gave me time to think. And then he said, 'So, can I bill you for new brake pads? I'm riding these brakes pretty hard.'"

"Sounds as if he has a good sense of humor."

"The best. He's very witty, Tams. Actually, he's very just about everything good that might have a 'very' put in front of it."

"Have you been to his house yet?"

"It's a condo in the sky. A loft really. Twenty-one stories up."

"Wow. That must be one of the tallest buildings in the city."

"It is. Every window has a great view. He even has a fireplace. Actually two fireplaces. But that isn't all."

"Tell, tell."

"He has the entire top floor."

"Impressive."

"And that still isn't all."

"What more?"

"He owns the entire building—or at least is the owner on the mortgage."

"I think I need to come down there and meet this guy. He does not sound like any sort of mailman I've ever met or heard about. Are you *sure* he's a mailman."

"Of course. He delivered my mail for months and months—like clockwork. Rain, sleet, snow, the whole mailman consistency."

"You sound a little hesitant. Don't you *want* me to meet him?"

"Sure. I really *do*, Tams. The only problem with that is I don't know precisely when he's going to be here next. He said that he is going to be here *for sure* for his birthday, but that's not for six weeks."

"No trip home before then?"

"I don't know. Maybe."

"So, Peter is gone. Lance is heading out for a few days, or weeks. We're both home alone."

"Where's Lance going?"

"Portland," said Tams.

"Funny," said Molly. "That's where Peter is going."

"Lance said something about Maine."

"Oh. Peter's Portland is in Oregon."

"Well, I'm not coming down there just to see *you*," Tams said. "Although we could have fun like two little mice while the cats are away."

"And your girls?"

"Oh, right. Motherhood. I just always assume that where I go, they go."

"That would be fine with me! I love being Aunt Molly."

"One of them is staring at me right now with that 'M-o-m' look. Gotta go."

"Later."

Molly did a few house chores, making sure her house was up to a potential dinner at *her* place if that's what Peter wanted to do on a Saturday night. Then she got dressed and at 12:50, the designated time, she called Grams. It wasn't just a ruse. They really did plan a fabulous birthday party for Peter.

"Let's keep all this a surprise," Grams suggested.

"Fine with me," Molly said. "But Peter knows we're planning a party . . . ."

"He doesn't know we're planning an extravaganza," Grams replied. "I should talk to Ed about this before we go much further in the planning."

"Right."

Molly hung up the phone with a huge smile. *Ellen would say it is of Cheshire proportions,* she thought. Grams was fun to talk to, fun to conspire with, and very much on her side.

When Peter came to pick her up, he was in the Lexus. It would be her first trip in the two-seater.

"Red pick-up yesterday, Lexus today," Molly said. "A chauffer tomorrow?"

"Actually, yes," Peter said. "That is, if you'll go to church with me in the morning and then to the club for brunch after."

"I will," said Molly. "I was just teasing about the chauffer."

"I wasn't," Peter said. "It makes get-away from church and getting-in at the club a whole lot more convenient."

"They'll expect you to put more in the offering plate."

"That's why I thought we'd go to your church," Peter said. "They probably won't expect too much on my first Sunday there."

There was an idea she hadn't anticipated. "Sure!" she said. "I'd love it if we went to my church. But I usually help teach Sunday school at nine. Church is at ten. We don't get out until about eleven-twenty."

"Fine with me. What age are the kids in your Sunday school class?"

"Ten, eleven. Girls. Fifth graders, actually. There's an adult class you could attend."

"You don't think I could handle girls ten and eleven years old?"

"Well . . . ."

"Let's see. There once was a girl named Molly who had a friend named . . . what was it . . . Tams?"

"I'll be ready at 8:30. I like to be there about 8:45 to help set up some things."

"And right now—I'm feeling a huge need to run on the treadmill at my gym. Want to go with me?"

"Will they let me in?"

"They will if I tell them you're with me."

"Let me grab some exercise clothes."

They spent an hour or so at the gym, and afterward, stopped by the computer store to check on an accessory that had caught Peter's attention.

And then, he suggested they go to a very nice steak house about fifteen miles out of town. "It's a four-star spa and it's very good, or so they tell me," he said. "Organic. Outstanding chef. It's called the Cornell Creek Inn."

"Sounds fancy," Molly said. She had never heard of the Cornell Creek Inn, but then again, she didn't often go out with her friends to four-star spas in the countryside.

"I think the food is the fancy part; the people and setting are New Age chic, or so they tell me." Then, noticing Molly's raised eyebrows he added, "Whatever New Age chic might mean."

"I have no clue. Probably no deep fry, and extra sprouts on the salads."

"Well, if they don't want my money, we'll come back and get ribs."

The Cornell Creek Inn was more modern than Molly had anticipated, the staff was relaxed, and the food was fabulous. It wasn't at all the no-red-meat-served place she had envisioned. Her steak, however, had been a Halibut steak. "I don't know who 'they' are—the people who told you about this place," Molly said, "but they have good taste."

"Sterilyn, actually," Peter said.

"How did your meeting go with her?" Molly asked.

"I learned what I needed to learn."

"Can you give me any clues as to why you needed to meet with her?"

"I wanted to ask her opinion about a financial deal," Peter said. It was true, just not exactly in the vein he knew Molly was envisioning. "I think I told you that Sterilyn comes from big money."

"But why have your grandmother in another room?" Molly asked. "Surely your grandmother . . . alright . . . *Grams* is highly conversant about financial deals."

"Absolutely. I don't know anybody who is quite as savvy as Grams when it comes to money. She didn't always have money, you know. Her grandfather and father had a way of making money only to lose money only to make more money. It was fortunate for her that her dad died on an upswing. Her grandfather had died on a downswing. I know Grams would have loved to hear what Sterilyn had to say, but Sterilyn is the private one when it comes to money talk. I knew she wouldn't open up completely if Grams was in the room."

"There a reason for that, I suppose?"

"Sterilyn doesn't really want people evaluating her decisions about money."

"And there's a reason for *that*, I suppose."

"She told me one time that some people gave her the impression that she was 'piling on' if she seemed to have money. Sterilyn knows she's a knock-out. She works hard at her figure and her face has always been in the natural-beauty category. She dresses well. And having money made her just 'too much,' she said for nice guys to ask her out or for girls to want to be her friend. In her terms, 'they don't think they can keep up.'"

"Making real friends isn't always as easy as some people think."

"Very true. I also think Sterilyn wants people to think she's smart—perhaps smarter than she actually is. I'm not saying that she's an airhead. Not at all. She's intelligent. But she isn't intelligent enough to have earned all that she has if she had started with zero. She can barely ride the wave of what she's worth. But she doesn't want people to know that. She likes for people to think that she's earning her way through life. It gives her validity, or credibility . . . or some other kind of undefined ability."

"But she obviously opens up to you."

"She sees me as potential happily-ever-after family—because of Ian. She thinks I have lots more money than I have, so that makes me more of an equal in her eyes. She was quite candid with me, actually, about the very things I wanted to know."

"What exactly did you want to know?" Molly asked. "Or, is that off limits?"

"Oh, things like Swiss bank accounts and off-shore tax-evasion schemes and . . . ."

"Stop teasing," Molly said. "I *don't* want to know!"

At least I hope he's teasing, she thought.

I hope she thinks I'm teasing, he thought.

At Molly's, they cranked up her stereo and moved the kitchen table to one side and had their own spontaneous dance-a-thon. It started as a dare and ended in exhausted laughter.

It had been a good day, and Sunday was almost a repeat—of goodness, that is.

The fifth-grade girls at First Church were enthralled with Peter. He was everything a prince charming should be, and they were both envious and happy for their teacher Molly. She was proud to have him sitting beside her in church, and was quite impressed with his good hymn-singing voice—a little harmony, even—and with the fact that he could say The Lord's Prayer without looking at the words in the bulletin.

"You know your way around a church service," she said later.

"I've gone to church all my life," Peter said.

"A family tradition?"

"Well, yes, I guess so. But one I like. One I do. I am a Christian, Molly," Peter said with great seriousness. "You knew that, right?"

"Lots of people call themselves Christian," Molly said, not entirely sure she wanted to pursue the conversation.

"Call?"

"I didn't mean that the way it sounded. It's just . . . a lot of people . . . ."

"I think I know where you're headed," said Peter. "That's why I don't talk about it. I believe. And I live out what I believe. That's my approach."

"It's mine, too," said Molly.

"You seem a little shy on this subject," said Peter.

"I am," said Molly, "and frankly, I don't know why. It seems like people can talk about the most intimate things these days—and sometimes the most bizarrely intimate things. They don't care who hears or knows. Just listen to the talk shows on TV. People admit to all sorts of beliefs and behaviors. But when it comes to a relationship with God, that's suddenly a no-talking zone."

"I think people will admit to being spiritual. Maybe even admit to having a relationship with God—or maybe the 'higher power' or the 'big man upstairs' or whatever."

"But then if you say Jesus . . . ."

"You're right. That's the big shut down. But not with me. We can talk about Jesus all you want."

"Why do you think people are quick to say they believe in God but they don't want to say they are tight with Jesus?"

"Probably because people are judgmental?" Peter asked rhetorically. "Or maybe because they think the person who claims to be a Christian is going to be judgmental."

"I think you're right," said Molly. "I don't want to judge. And I don't want to be judged.

"But what you believe is at the heart of who you are," Peter said. "I've known that from the first hour I was with you at the New Year's party."

"How did you know?"

"I just did. Your beliefs play out in the way you talk—the words you *don't* say, the jokes and gossip you *don't* want to overhear, boundaries of your morality, the concerns you have for other people . . . ."

"Am I that transparent?"

"Yes," said Peter. "And we wouldn't be sitting here together right now if you weren't that transparent. I'm not interested in relationships that are guessing-games . . . or in relationships that have some sort of sliding scale of beliefs."

"You're rare, Peter Lorgham," Molly said softly. "Very rare."

"Maybe. I don't feel rare—more like medium. Maybe medium *well*."

"Cute."

"The metaphor works. I find it very comforting—and also very exciting—that I can be myself with you, and that I feel as if you are being totally yourself with me. No games. No deep dark secret sins. No manipulation . . . *especially* no manipulation."

"I feel the same way."

"So there you have it. Two squares. Two Christians. Trying to be hip and modern. But also trying to keep things right."

After that, what could Molly do? She had to tell him what she knew about the activities at the house with grey trim.

"There's something I need to tell you, Peter," Molly began, with a little hesitation, "in the interest of total transparency."

"I have a couple of things I should probably tell you, too," Peter said.

"Okay, you first," Molly said.

"Actually, I'd like to hear you out," Peter said. "It might give me more courage."

"Well . . ." began Molly, "it has to do with the house with grey trim."

Peter leaned forward. "Please tell me you didn't go there," Peter said.

"Not directly," Molly replied. "Actually, I *personally* didn't even go there indirectly."

She then told Peter in detail about what Ellen had observed in the back yard of the house with grey trim. To her surprise, Peter didn't seem either upset, or doubtful. She had expected a little of both, and said so.

"I knew things were going on there," Peter said quietly. "Let's go back to your house. The things we are sharing tonight just might be things that should not be overheard."

Once back at the house, with mugs of hot tea in hand, Peter said, "I don't think I've overtly lied to you, Molly, but I also know that I haven't been entirely truthful with you—not in the sense of the whole truth, nothing but the truth, so help me God."

"Please don't tell me you are married with kids," Molly said.

Peter laughed. "No, nothing like that." And then quickly added, "Are *you*?"

"No," Molly said. "But I've heard that same preface speech from a guy who *was* married with kids. It was just a minor detail that he forgot to tell me about during the first three months we dated."

"Well, that isn't it," said Peter.

Molly waited in silence.

"The truth is that I'm not just your mailman," said Peter.

"What does that mean, 'not just?'"

"I've delivered your mail—for lots of months—but that was really an under-cover job I've had with the government," said Peter. "I might lose my real job in telling you this—if anybody ever found out that you know. And please know this, too—you could be in serious danger if the people at Gray Tudor, which is what I call the house with grey trim, ever connected you to me."

"And your real job is . . . ?" asked Molly, feigning a drumroll.

"F.B.I."

Molly sunk more deeply in her chair. She usually had a pretty good poker face when it came to receiving surprise news, but not this time.

"What is it that you think is going on at Gray Tudor," she asked.

"We think it is a link in a fairly extensive prostitution ring—and more specifically, trafficking teenage girls as sex slaves."

"I saw a TV show on that recently, but it never dawned on me things like that could happen in a neighborhood like mine."

"That's part of the reason it has worked for so long and so successfully," Peter said. "The slave-owners, or pimps, or crooks—whatever you want to call them—hook up with very young teenagers who are feeling bullied and underappreciated at home, school, and by society as a whole. They befriend these girls—some of them are only eleven or twelve years old. They buy nice things for them, talk about how they could be super models if they just had the right training, and next thing you know, the girls have gone to a place like Gray Tudor to live. They think they are entering a higher level of society that will also be a 'finishing school,' of sorts, to help them become models."

"Interesting that you would use the word 'finishing,'" said Molly.

"No wit intended," Peter said. "But you are right in your inference. For most of the girls, moving into Gray Tudor is the first step down an irreversible slippery slope."

"What happens to them?"

"At first, the so-called 'training' goes on in a fairly innocent and certainly enticing manner. The girls get new clothes, make-up classes, new hairdos, a photo shoot with a guy who appears to be a real pro—and may actually be a real pro. The girls are taken to nice restaurants and high-class clubs. Then the drugs start. Just a little at first. Nothing to spook the girls away."

Peter paused for a few seconds and then continued, "Before they know it, the girls are involved sexually with their benefactors, usually at the beginning with the use of a date-rape drug of some kind that lowers any inhibitions the girl might have. The girls, for the most part, are virgins or very inexperienced going in. Maybe they've had sex with a guy their age, or a little older, but no involvement with a man in his thirties who knows all the right things to say and do."

"And once a girl is in the clutches of a pimp?" Molly asked.

"He suggests that they take a trip."

"Where to?"

"From here, the road seems to lead to San Francisco, and then a road trip north through Bend, Oregon, and over to Portland."

"So that's why you are going to Portland," Molly said.

"Yes."

"No efficiency for the postal service on the horizon."

"Not at this particular time," said Peter.

"It would be good to have more efficiency," Molly said. And then turning directly to Peter she added, "This makes me very concerned for your safety."

"Nobody ever told me that working for the F.B.I. would be a walk in the park," Peter said matter-of-factly. "But I'm not in much danger, as long as I remain invisible to these guys."

"What happens in Portland?" Molly asked.

"That's where things spin out of control, from the girls' standpoint. There's a major ring of guys who appear to be wealthy businessmen—some of them Oriental, some Caucasian. They tell the girls that international model jobs are awaiting them in Thailand. Most of the girls go willingly. If a girl resists, she is plied with more drugs and money before putting her hands on a plane ticket. Along the way, the pimp gets a passport—and that is presented to the girl as a good-faith gift. The girls are told they can come home any time they want."

"Which is a lie," deduced Molly.

"And like all lies, is fairly easily swallowed once a girl has gone that far down the road to the Orient."

"How do you know all this?" Molly said. "*Some* girl *somewhere* must have come home."

"Actually, a local father cared enough to go after his daughter. A friend of this guy saw the girl on an international porn website. The friend traveled to Thailand and Malaysia fairly often, in legit business, and one of his contacts there offered him his choice of young girls on a Thai website—as an 'escort' for a night out in Bangkok. The friend said he had a headache . . . ."

"You're kidding," interrupted Molly. "A *headache*?"

"I know, I know." said Peter. "But it was true in this case. The onset of his headache wasn't as severe as he claimed it was, but he definitely was starting to develop a headache after seeing the variety of girls who might be his 'escort.' The guy had suffered from migraines for years and had the meds in his briefcase to prove it. He told our guys he didn't think any of the girls in the website photos were over fifteen. The business contact in Thailand let him off the hook, and never suspected anything."

"The good news for us," Peter continued, "was that the guy was clear-headed enough to write down the name of the website. When he got back to the States a few days later, he showed the website to the father, who, by the way, had not seen his daughter in a couple of years. Nasty divorce, no visitation rights, lots of lies from his ex in both directions—both to the dad and to the girl. He called his ex, then he called us, and then we helped him verify that the girl on the website really was his daughter. There were some questions about that, as you might imagine. A girl can really change in looks between ages eleven and thirteen, especially with the help of some heavy make-up and hairstyle changes. Then we worked out a deal with the C.I.A. to do a sting operation in Bangkok."

"And she was freed?"

"Yes," said Peter, "and glad to be free. Some of the girls don't want to come home. At least not at first."

"Why not?"

"The drugs have a real hold on them."

"What do you do?"

"We bring them home anyway—if at all possible. And then they face some serious detox in a hospital, all underground. Then we try to give them new identities. We did that for the girl I just told you about—detox and a new identity. She needed several months of psychotherapy. That's a part of the process."

"Can this entire thing be shut down?" Molly asked. "It seems to have lots of raw edges."

"You're absolutely right in your analysis," Peter said with admiration in his voice. "It's an issue that's broad and deep and jagged and cloaked in secrecy, drugs, and porn. What we can hope for is a clearer picture of who is doing what so we can target the real points of vulnerability in the sex-trade route, and then perhaps in a few weeks, pull all stops to conduct raids in several states—and countries— simultaneously."

Molly got up to get herself a glass of water and said as she made her way down the hall toward her bedroom, "I think I need to get some headache medication." Then added, "Just kidding!"

When she returned to the living room she made herself a second cup of tea and said, "Is that it? You're F.B.I. and you're involved in a potentially very dangerous assignment of helping bring down a sex-trade prostitution ring that is operating in Thailand and also in my neighborhood."

"That's mostly it," said Peter.

"I was trying to be flip. This is pretty mind-blowing, Peter," said Molly. "So—what more do you have to tell me?"

"The packet Carvill found in his flowerbed . . . ."

"Don't tell me that has something to do with Gray Tudor!"

"No, entirely different," said Peter.

"I think I need to move."

"Maybe," said Peter.

"You're *serious?*" Molly replied.

"Depends on what shakes down."

"Okay, back to the torn-up envelope that had the Miss Peacock brooch in it . . . ."

"I don't think it was mailed to Carvill at all," said Peter.

"No?"

"No," said Peter. "I looked closely at what was left of the address on the envelope. The street name had been chewed off but the last three numbers of the address were still there. 7-6-2.

That's the last part of Carvill's address. He's 3762. But there's another house in the neighborhood that has the last digits 7-6-2, two streets over. That usually doesn't happen in a neighborhood but in this case, it happened. I think it has something to do with the fact that what we both think of as *one* neighborhood now, was actually two different developments forty years ago, and when the little bridge was put in over the creek, things melded together. Anyway, I've almost shuffled mail with an address ending 7-6-2 into the wrong slot at the sorting table. No delivery mistakes on my watch, however—truth is, Carvill's mail is mostly junk and circulars. The other address doesn't get very much mail at all."

"So you think this packet was intended for delivery at the *other* 7-6-2 address?"

"I do."

"And which house is that?" Molly asked.

"The house directly across the cul-de-sac from your new friend Ellen."

"The Christmas Deco Depot?" asked Molly.

"Yes."

"Good grief," said Molly. "It's a crime wave." Then, in a completely serious tone of voice she asked, "So what do you think is going on in that house?"

"I've just started putting some pieces together," said Peter, "but given what we *both* know at this point, I'm guessing that this may be an operation that involves the fencing of stolen goods, and maybe even money laundering."

"So somebody ships or delivers stolen goods to the house, and then they are reshipped to somebody else?"

"Right. Guy at the Christmas Deco Depot gets a cut along the way. He's the one with the contacts. And he may not be the only guy in the middle. It could all be part of a bigger scheme to throw off all suspicion."

"Why not just call the cops and have them go in with a search warrant?" Molly asked.

"If the stolen merchandise is being sent across state lines, it becomes an F.B.I. matter. For that matter, unauthorized or illegal use of Post Office mail also makes it a federal offense— assuming at this point that the Post Office is involved in some way. Or, maybe UPS falls under the same code. And, since a couple of boxes I once spotted on the doorstep of that house had international UPS address forms attached to them, it could also end up involving the C.I.A. A piece like Grams' peacock would be a high-priced article in any legit art or jewelry market. I have put out some queries through my sources to UPS and to a couple of banks."

"Banks? Money laundering?" asked Molly, trying to stay up with all that Peter was saying in his rather meandering monolog.

"I hadn't thought of the money-laundering angle until I was rethinking my conversation with Sterilyn about off-shore and international banking. The money laundering may not be part of what's happening at the Christmas house, but then again, it might be."

"And, of course, I can't say a word about any of this to Ellen," said Molly.

"Not even one syllable. About either Gray Tudor or the Christmas house."

"Shouldn't she be warned?"

"Warned of what?"

"The potential danger of getting spotted or getting involved. What if she stumbles blindly into something?"

"If she suggests any more sleuthing with the loose brick in her backyard fence, discourage her," said Peter.

"I don't think that will happen," Molly said. "The brick part of the fence was on the side of Gray Tudor. Her wood-slat fence was fixed by her husband."

"Good," said Peter. "And as for the Christmas house, keep walking when the guy isn't around."

"One thing about all that—if somebody stole, or found, Grams' brooch and then mailed it to the Christmas house, won't that person be wondering why he hasn't heard anything or received any money?"

"I suspect the thief is just now starting to wonder that," said Peter. "My guess is that he forgot to keep the address and it will take him a day or so to follow up."

Molly suddenly sat up straight and said with urgency, "You don't think the marijuana is being shipped out of the Christmas Deco Depot, do you?"

"I hope not," said Peter. "Hadn't thought of that. I like old man Epstein. I wish there was a way out of that situation for him that didn't involve law enforcement at any level."

"Do you think he might be convinced to get rid of the plants—like, on his own, before anybody could turn him in?" Molly ventured.

"That's an idea worth considering. I'm open to all suggestions," said Peter.

When Molly didn't respond immediately he asked, "Do you *have* an idea?"

"No," said Molly, "but I'm wondering about something that is probably going to seem like a total disconnect to you."

"What?"

"How do you feel about prayer? Do you think it makes any difference?"

"Are you asking me if I think God can give somebody a good idea after that person prays and asks for a good idea?"

"Yeah, something like that," said Molly.

"Actually, I do believe that," said Peter. "I also think that God hears prayers asking for protection and for the destruction of evil forces."

"Me, too," said Molly. Turning to look Peter directly in the eyes, she said, "Do you think we have a strong enough friendship, Peter Lorgham, that we might consider praying together—or would that just derail everything?"

Peter smiled. "I think we can survive praying together."

And so they did. They prayed about Peter's work in Portland . . . about the girls who had been sucked into the cesspool drain of Gray Tudor . . . and that the truth might be revealed about the activities of the Christmas Deco Depot. They prayed that Mr. Epstein might be spared legal action, and that both Peter and Molly would have wisdom and be kept safe.

By the time they said "amen," the clock said four-thirty. "I have to leave for the airport in an hour," Peter said. "So much for sleep."

"I can't believe we talked all night. Can I make a little breakfast for you before you leave?"

"Thanks, but I'll grab something at the airport," Peter said. And then as he approached the front door he suddenly turned and said, "I almost forgot, there's something else I meant to tell you tonight."

"Nothing too major, I hope," said Molly. "We've already talked the night away on the subjects at hand!"

"Actually, it's more major than anything we've talked about," said Peter.

"What?" said Molly.

She was totally unprepared for Peter to take her face in his hands, kiss her, and then say, "I love you, Molly Herman."

24

"Brilliant!" Molly said aloud, and loudly, as she threw back the covers on her bed and nearly jumped from her bed—all of which sent Houndcat flying and mewing in angry disgust.

"Sorry," said Molly. "But some ideas are just that good."

Later that day, she stopped by the store to get baking supplies, and the following day, she paid a visit to Mr. Epstein with a three-level frosted cake in hand.

"You don't know me," she said when Mr. Epstein answered the door, "but I'm one of your neighbors. The woman next door to me told me that you grow orchids. I was given a potted orchid at Christmastime, and I really need some advice. I asked the flower shop up the street and the gal there was not the normal saleslady and she said she didn't have a clue. 'We just sell 'em, we don't grow 'em.' Those were her exact words. So . . . I'm here on your doorstep. And I brought a homemade cake as a down-payment on whatever advice you can give me."

The tale was not a total lie. Molly had been given a fairly tall and extremely beautiful potted orchid by her boss. And, it was true that she did not know how to care for it, especially now that it had started losing a blossom or two. She clothed her speech with as much charm as possible.

"Do you know what kind of orchid it is?"

"No," fibbed Molly. She knew perfectly well the name the florist used for the orchid, but she suspected that giving Mr. Epstein such information would not further her plan. "I'm pretty sure, though, if you are growing several different varieties of orchids, and if one of those varieties was the same as my plant, I'd recognize it."

"Good idea," said Mr. Epstein, "if you don't mind walking through the house of a stranger to my greenhouse out back."

"I trust you," said Molly, moving into the house as he held the door open for her."

"Ignore the mess you see along the way," said Mr. Epstein. "I'm an old widower, you know. Can't be bothered with too much housekeeping. You put stuff away and then you just have to haul it out again, and then put it away again. So, I just leave it all *out!*"

He led the way across the living room, and through the dining room to a back door that was only a few flagstone steps away from the entrance to his greenhouse. She noted that he took a ring of keys from a hook by the back door, and then used one of those keys to open the locked greenhouse.

The greenhouse was filled with several dozen orchid plants and even more African violets. "Oh my!" Molly exclaimed. "You have the most beautiful backyard I've ever seen!"

"I'm up to 67 orchids now," Mr. Epstein said proudly. "Forty-eight varieties. The amazing thing about *Orchidaceae* is that the plants come in so many varieties—with different shapes and colors of flowers—and all of them beautiful."

"Amazing," said Molly, trying to take in the floral grandeur before her. "Did you say '*Orchidaceae*?'"

"That's the official word for the orchid family—monocots in the order *Asparagales*."

"Oh," said Molly, fully aware that Mr. Epstein was showing off, but glad to be the audience for his lecture nonetheless.

"Yep," Mr. Epstein continued. "Probably about 25,000 species of orchids—and just for the record, that makes *Orchidaceae* the second largest family of flowing plants on earth. There are twice the number of orchid species as bird species and four times the number of mammal species. And even so, orchids are rare in these parts. Too cold for them. Although there are some types of orchids that live near Antarctica."

"You have obviously studied this. Do you teach this subject?"

"Only to neighbors in need," said Mr. Epstein. "In my former life, I was a botany teacher at the college up the road."

"Oh, is it Dr. Epstein, then?" Molly asked.

"Technically, I suppose it is," Dr. Epstein asked. "But it's been a long time since anybody called me that. Most folks just call me Ernie, which I certainly invite you—as my neighbor—to do."

Molly continued moving from plant to plant. "There it is!" she said with exuberance.

"Ah, the *Phalaenopsis lindenii,*" said Ernie "Delicate and beautiful. Popular cultivated plant."

In surveying the orchids and violets, of course, Molly had spotted several large trays of hemp plants in a variety of sizes.

"Dr. Epstein," she said in feigned surprise, "do you know what these plants are?" And then, also feigning a realization that her host, a notable botanist, would most certainly know the species at hand, she added, "But I guess as a botanist . . . ."

"Sure," he said, not at all embarrassed about the plants in question. "*Cannabis sativa.* Also known as hemp. Also known as marijuana. Also known as pot."

"Are you doing research on them . . . as a botanist, I mean?" Molly asked

"No," Ernie laughed. "Most of the necessary research on these babies was done in the 1960's, I think."

"Is it . . . uh . . . legal . . . for you to be growing all these plants?" Molly asked, and then quickly followed up her question by saying, "You don't need to answer that if you don't want to. I'm really embarrassed I asked . . . ."

My drama teacher in high school would be very impressed, Molly thought, evaluating her own performance in conversing with Dr. Ernest Epstein.

"Actually, it is legal," said Dr. Epstein. "I'm glad you recognized the plants for what they are, and glad you asked. I would hate to think you had spotted the plants, knew what they were, and went away thinking your neighbor Epstein was a crook."

"So . . . you . . . are . . . ?" Molly asked haltingly. She truly did not know how to finish the question. She couldn't think of anything apart from research that sounded legal.

"I have a license—see, posted right there by the door, that I am one of three growers in our state who can produce marijuana for medicinal processing."

"Oh, wow," Molly said softly.

Looking through the greenhouse toward the back fence, she saw a large hedge of hemp, and turned with wide eyes to Ernie. "And those are the same, only massive."

"Right," said Ernie. "Harvest is in two weeks."

"A pharmaceutical company right here in the ol' neighborhood," Molly said. "And orchids and violets, too."

"One species for smoking. One for beauty. And one for giving away to those I help in the hospitals where I volunteer. All of them probably address the issue of pain at some point in some way."

Molly nodded with appreciation and her host continued, "I sell the babies from the orchids. I sell the entire hemp plants. I'm making more in my retirement than I ever did as a professor," Ernie said with pride, and then added, "My grandson got me into the pot business."

No doubt, thought Molly.

"Ernie 3. I'm Ernie and his dad is Ernie 2. Ernie 3's mom has a very rare nerve disease—the ends of her nerves are fraying and are inflamed. A tremendously painful condition. Docs figure her pain is somewhere around 12 on a 10-point scale. And its nonstop. Nothing but the strongest opiates can give her any relief—that is, other than pot. It really helps." Dr. Epstein puttered among the plants of his greenhouse—removing a few dead leaves, training up a few orchid stalks against green stakes.

He continued talking as he worked, glad to have an attentive and pretty woman interested in what he had to say. "Ernie 3 came to me one day and told me he had been reading about medicinal uses of marijuana. Poor kid had tears in his eyes. 'Can't you grow her some, Grandpa?' he asked. What could I say?"

"Just what you said," Molly offered.

"First I had to find a way to do it legally. Made a few calls. Visited a few bureaucrats in their offices. Talked to some people I had known through the college. Got the license. Found a good source for the plants. And here we are. I've been growing and harvesting for a couple of years now."

"And how is your daughter-in-law doing?"

"The disease is still progressing," Ernie said. "Docs don't hold out any hope for a cure. She's smoking a joint a day. I'm glad that gives her a little relief."

"Are you ever nervous about having so much pot growing in your backyard? Do any of the neighbors know about it?" Molly asked.

"You mean, nervous that my plants might be stolen?"

"Right," said Molly. "I didn't ask that very well."

"I've thought about it. But I think beyond *you*—and I'm certainly hoping I can trust you . . . ."

"Yes, indeed," said Molly. "My lips are sealed."

"Beyond you, the only person who knows anything about it is the guy across the back fence. He's a weird one, but I don't think he's going to turn me in."

"What do you mean, a weird one?" Molly asked.

"Have you ever seen his house? Never takes down his Christmas paraphernalia," said Ernie. "Not that I know much about all that—I'm Jewish. You might have figured that out from my name. But it doesn't seem that any of my other neighbors who celebrate Christmas leave up their doo-dahs all year."

"No, that is pretty strange, alright," said Molly, again feigning innocence on the subject of the Christmas Deco Depot. "Do you think he knows about the pot?"

"Sure of it," said Ernie. "I see little branches and leaves stripped off occasionally. Lower to the ground. Branches that have grown close to the chain-link fence. Not a lot missing, but a little—a joint's worth, I'm thinking, once the leaves and hard wood are dried."

"You don't think he'll turn you in?"

"Not really. I don't think a man who leaves his Christmas stuff up all year would want too many legal types snooping around. Plus, I'm glad he hires Ernie 3 to do his yard. If I was growing tomatoes and a vine grew close enough for him to pick a tomato occasionally, I wouldn't mind."

"Good neighbor," said Molly. "But then, tomatoes aren't illegal."

"I'm legal. If he gets caught with a joint of his own making, he's the one in possession," said Ernie. "I'm not too worried."

"You don't think he might do a little more harvesting and sell your profits?" Molly asked. "Actually, it's none of my business . . . ."

"Interesting point. But I don't think so. He's weird, but I don't think he's either dangerous or a serious thief. He's only at that house a few hours a day and never any parties or people coming and going. Ernie 3 says the only people he's ever seen at the house, other than the guy working inside, are the UPS drivers who drop off and pick up boxes."

"Has Ernie 3 ever actually seen the owner?" Molly asked. "My friend Ellen lives across the cul-de-sac from that house and she told me one time she doesn't think anybody lives there."

"Yeah, Ernie has seen the guy. He wears a blonde wig. Ernie thinks he might . . . how can I say this without being too politically incorrect . . . he might like to wear women's clothes."

"Oh," said Molly. And then with a laugh she added, "Weird, alright."

Changing subjects, Molly made a strong pitch to legitimize all her curiosity and too-lengthy stay. "Can you give me some advice about my orchid?"

"What are you wanting to do with it?"

"Well, for one, keep it alive."

"I suggest that you bring it around next Sunday, maybe. I try to keep Saturday special, you know. But then again, you might have that feeling about Sunday. How about if you come over about this time next Monday afternoon? We'll take a look and see what might be done. Maybe you'll be able to propagate it—have baby orchids."

"Now there's an idea I hadn't thought about!" Molly said. "Maybe I should think about having a greenhouse of my own."

"Not unless you want a lot of work," said Ernie, with a twinkle in his eyes. "I couldn't do any of this until after I retired."

At last, Molly thought as she walked home, *a neighbor whose mystery has a really good ending.* She could hardly wait to tell Peter.

25

The weekend was filled with good phone calls. Peter had called in a relaxed mood and they had talked for almost two hours—about events in their past, people they called their friends, Molly's sister, Peter's brother, what they thought, and even current events. In the rapid flow of conversation, she had forgotten to tell Peter about Dr. Epstein, but oh well . . . another day, another conversation.

Molly was pleased that Peter was missing her, and that he had made some progress on his "project" in Portland. He told her he was working closely with some top-flight computer experts. "They are really good," he said. "All of them are under twenty-one."

"Good and under twenty-one?" Molly asked. "Did I hear you right?"

"Nobody that is really top-flight in computer hacking and analysis is over twenty-one," Peter said matter-of-factly. "When I meet guys like these, I'm always very glad they are on our side."

Peter had ended the call with a light but sincere, "I love you, Molly."

She had responded only, "I'm glad!" It had always been a big step for her to admit to any man that she felt *love* for him. But she was also sure that in the near future, she would probably find herself using the "L" word in confessing her feelings to Peter Lorgham.

"He's just amazing," she had said to Tams, who called within minutes after her call ended with Peter.

"I'm assuming that you are taking about Prince Peter," Tams replied.

"Who?" asked Molly.

"Oh, alright, I'll just have to call him Peter, I guess. No Petie-Eye, no Prince Peter. Just plain ol' Peter. How did your weekend end with him?"

Molly laughed.

"Nothing plain ol' about him," Molly said. "The adjectives and nicknames just don't do him justice. He's really amazing."

"What has he done now?"

Molly knew she couldn't give any details about their conversation the previous weekend, but she tell Tams that they had gone to church together on Sunday. "And the most wonderful thing, Tams . . . Peter is a Christian."

"Isn't everybody?" Tams said with a fair amount of cynicism. "I mean, don't most people say they are?"

"He's a real one, Tams. Like the people we knew as kids at the church on Cottonwood Road."

"You talked about God?" Tams was genuinely surprised.

"We did."

"That's pretty intense."

"Not really. At least it didn't seem overly intense. It just seemed normal."

"That is amazing," Tams said. And then, with a great overtone of reflection, she said, "It's strange, isn't it, Molly, that people will talk about everything but God? I have a friend here who has been dating a guy for seven or eight months. I asked her if he went to church and she said she didn't know."

"Do you think she wanted to know?"

"Probably not. When she said that she didn't know, she also said, 'That would be pretty personal to talk about.' Pretty personal? I thought to myself, She's probably having sex with this guy and she thinks it is too personal to ask him if he ever goes to church? We live in a strange world, Molly."

"I know. And for the record, I am *not* having sex with Peter and he *does* go to church regularly. And . . . we even prayed together before he kissed me goodnight on Sunday."

"Wow," Tams said. "This is really happening."

"It was the most intimate I think I have ever been with a guy," Molly said quietly. "It's almost too wonderful to put into words."

"I *must* meet him," Tams said. "I think he's going to be the one."

"I'm thinking he just might be," said Molly. "And oh, by the way, he told me as he walked out the door that he loves me."

"He what?" Tams nearly shouted into the phone. "We've had this entire conversation and you're just now telling me that?"

Molly laughed.

"Was it luvya? Or love you? Or a real, 'I love you'?" asked Tams.

"Does it make a difference?"

"Huge difference."

"The latter. Three words and my name."

"Yes, yes, yes," said Tams. "I can hear the wedding bells!"

"Don't get too excited," Molly cautioned.

"Ah no . . . don't tell me. You didn't admit that you love him, too . . . did you?"

"No."

167

"Ah, Molly. You need to *tell* him!"

"I need to know for sure, first."

"Well then I'm going to hang up and let you get on with figuring it out!" said Tams.

Five minutes later, Mrs. Glossman phoned. "Molly, dear," she said, "I talked to Edgar. Carvill that is. And he is one hundred percent on board with our idea."

Molly chuckled. Grams picked up on the reason. "Oh dear, I really said 'on board,' didn't I?"

"I thought it was very clever," Molly said. And then quickly added, "I'm very excited he agreed!"

"He even seemed a bit excited. Poor ol' chap probably hasn't been involved in anything like this for a while."

"What's the next thing I should be doing?"

"You should check your calendar to see if we might have dinner at the club on Thursday. Or Friday is open, too."

"I have my calendar right here. Yes, either night works for me."

"Alright, then. I'll meet you at the club at seven o'clock on Thursday. Bring your calendar or notepad or something. I have a hunch that we can have this nailed down before we get to dessert."

"I believe we can! I'll see you then."

Molly was pleased . . . about virtually everything. *Life is beautiful!* she thought. And then as if she had been hit by a bolt of lightning, she concluded, *I'm in love! Life is just not this beautiful without it being love.* It was an idea that she savored.

I'm in love with my mailman! Well, at least he had been her mailman.

26

Lance listened to all Peter had to tell him, and then walked over to the tenth-story window that looked out over a significant portion of Portland.

"Are you sure?"

"I can doublecheck everything, but at this point, I'd say I'm more than ninety percent sure."

"You know," Lance mused, "this just might be connected to that interstate theft ring that was operating out of Des Moines, linked up to Ottawa and from there, to Europe. Similar M.O."

"My guess is that most of the stuff is 'small'— jewelry, small electronics, GPS units, that sort of thing. Although the neighbor seeing large boxes brought into the garage might signal something bigger. Second guess is that the end destination is always out of the States. Electronics have too many ID numbers that can be traced. The usual way of selling art and antique jewelry is pretty well documented—and even the F.B.I. is onto the use of Craig's List and e-bay."

"Let's get the necessary paperwork going for an approach to UPS, and plot a strategy that will do more than just shut down the guy on your mail run."

"Will do. Whatever the strategy, we don't want to spook him into moving from his current location. And, if he's part of a ring, let's get the entire ring. He doesn't appear to be dangerous, but who knows what kinds of weapons might be in the house . . . or what might tip him over. He's a little odd, I'd say."

"We're on the same page. I'll get the paperwork going for C.I.A. approvals."

Lance turned to look Peter in the eye. "You're about to tell me that Molly is the one who figured out a lot of this, aren't you?"

"No," said Peter, but then added, "but she does know about the brooch and the address possibility linking the mail packet to the house that has the Christmas decorations permanently installed."

"How did she get involved?" Lance asked. "I'm not interrogating you . . . just want to know in case I'm asked."

"She's the one who first saw my grandmother and the mangled envelope outside the Carvill residence. Her exercise pal is the woman who lives across the cul-de-sac from what she and her friend call the Christmas Deco Depot."

"That Christmas decorations deal is . . . well, most crooks don't like to call attention to themselves," Lance said. "That's one of the little pieces of all this that makes me wonder if the guy is just a legitimate buy-low-and-sell-high trader."

"That's one of the things I questioned, too," said Peter. "But then I talked to a couple of the kitchen staff employees at the country club. I've known them since I was a kid—used to raid the kitchen for scraps for my dogs. Johnny Lee and Wilbur both told me that they remembered my grandmother coming around to ask about her pin— their boss had asked them who had waited on Mrs. Glossman. They did their own little investigation and concluded that a new hire named Carlos had waited their table, and then one of them recalled that Carlos had picked up Mrs. Glossman's scarf from the floor and had brought it into the kitchen.

"Another waiter, Ybarra, had asked him what he was doing and he said that he had spilled something on the scarf and was going to try to wash it out. Which he apparently did, or pretended to do, and then returned the scarf. I figure that's when and how the brooch was lifted. Carlos later denied, of course, that there had been any jewelry on the scarf. He said he got the spot out of the scarf and took it back to the table. Johnny Lee said he acted a little nervous, but Johnny Lee figured that was owing solely to the fact that Carlos was afraid of being reprimanded for spilling something onto a member's clothing and then compounding his mistake by trying to cover for the accident. It's really against waiter rules, apparently, to attempt to clean a spot without the garment owner's permission."

"And none of the guests at your grandmother's table saw the scarf go or return?"

"No. Grams said she asked all her friends if they had seen the pin on her scarf. She told me, 'Some said yes, some said no.' She figured her friends didn't really know—they were all too busy talking and trying so hard to hear everything that everybody else was saying that they probably had no sense at all that anything abnormal was happening around them. Waiters come and waiters go. Water glasses get filled and plates get removed. A scarf picked up from the floor, tucked under a platter, and casually returned to the back of a chair as the next course is delivered . . . it all just happens, you know."

"And somehow this Carlos fellow got connected with somebody who knew that the brooch was studded with real jewels, and that the

Christmas guy was a good fence for something like that . . . ."

"I haven't been able to confirm that assumption or make that connection," said Peter. "I'm guessing that Carlos didn't really know the value of the brooch—if he had, he probably wouldn't have sent it by mail. I'm also guessing that he just wanted a few bucks from the sale of a rich lady's gaudy piece of jewelry, and that a friend of a friend might have said, 'I think I know a guy who might buy that from you.' Carlos is single and flexible—documented but probably only barely. At least I'm pretty sure that's his profile. If I'm right, that's probably the main reason he hasn't raised any objections, yet, as to why he hasn't heard back from Santa Claus."

"If he didn't really think the peacock was all that valuable, and he isn't fully documented . . . well, being found out isn't worth a few pin feathers, so to speak."

Peter smiled. Lance wasn't just one of the most logical C.I.A. operatives he had ever encountered, he was one of the most fun to work with.

"Got any ideas about how to shake some information from Carlos?" Lance asked.

"I was thinking that I'd ask Mario in our district office to put out some bait. Carlos might be willing to help a beautiful young senorita with a contact for selling some of her jewelry to pay her rent. That kind of thing."

"Sounds good. Nothing, though, that would send Carlos looking for the next bus out of town."

"Agreed. I'll get the paper work going on my end, and keep you posted."

"Now," said Lance, changing tone. "How am I going to explain that you came across all of this when you were supposed to be devoting your full attention to Sterilyn's deposition and to Gray Tudor."

"Life is a winding road," said Peter with a shrug. "Besides, I'm assuming that given the information I sent you two days ago, I'm out of the Sterilyn loop."

"For now. That was good stuff. Apparently just the right key for at least one locked door."

"Good."

"And Gray Tudor . . . have you met this Ellen person that Molly walks with?"

"No."

"So you don't know first-hand if we can trust her backyard peep-hole observations."

"No. But they line up with what we've been suspecting for months."

"We've got to find a way of knowing when Tudor Man goes out of town with his next girl."

"I think I have an idea," said Peter. "It might work—or might not. We've been assuming that Tudor Man keeps a girl about three to five weeks before he passes her off. I'm guessing that he drives these girls out of state on his own."

"What makes you think that?"

"Junk circulars—you know, the kind that are hung up on doorknobs or put on doormats. They used to pile up for three to four days at a time. And, I noticed that a different vehicle was sometimes parked in the driveway just before the junk-circulars phenomenon kicked in."

"Which led you to what conclusion?"

"I think this guy has a little side business of driving vehicles to out-of-state locations . . . *one way*. I had a buddy in college who earned good money by driving luxury cars one way for businessmen who wanted their own vehicle in a city where they were going to be working for several weeks or months. The business exec flew. My friend drove the car, and then flew home."

"Old economy," Lance noted. "Before recession."

"Right. The prosperous years when gas was cheap and time was everything and luxury cars weren't part of the rental-agency line-ups. For that matter, luxury cars were admired, not dissed for their carbon footprint."

"So, this guy times his girl deliveries to coincide with car deliveries?"

"Keeps anybody from questioning his trips. Gives him a free air ticket home. Pays for the freight, so to speak. And gives him an alibi—he can go to just about any destination in the general direction or vicinity of where he wants to end up, and then fly back without any suspicion."

"And the way to tell when he's about to make a delivery trip depends upon spotting an 'unknown' car in his driveway . . . ."

"I know that might sound like a long shot, but past surveillance of Gray Tudor confirmed what I suspected on my mail route. This guy doesn't have a lot of drop-in company. No parties. No frequent visitors. No guests who stay day after day. The unusual cars show up one afternoon and are gone the next morning. On one occasion, I saw the delivery of such a car—Mr. Tudor Man drove away with him and came back in the vehicle as the driver and sole occupant."

"Two-level surveillance, right?"

"Right. One level to detect the appearance of a new car in the driveway. Second level to detect departure time. I'm guessing that happens in the dark hours. Night-time surveillance needs to have two prongs. One focused on the house, and the other, a 24-7 car stationed nearby to pick up his trail the minute he pulls out of the driveway or garage. Once he's left the house, he's going to go *somewhere*. And we need to follow him all the way to Portland."

"And hope that he comes to Portland," said Lance. "Straight into mama's arms, so to speak."

"Right."

"Do you have the manpower for that kind of surveillance?"

"I think so," said Peter.

"How close do you think we are to his next delivery?"

"Close."

"Go for it," said Lance simply. "Anything else?"

I don't think I've told you about the cleaning service angle."

"No."

"I figured this guy is a *guy*, and he has to have a house that is presentable to the girls he brings home. He has to make an impression that he's not a slumlord, and also that he's not looking for a girl to be his maid. These are young girls, but they are also likely to be girls who have been ordered to do an unfair share of grunge work. They're going to be really sensitive to a messed-up house and the possibility that the guy who owns it is looking for somebody to clean toilets and mop floors. They're going to be even more impressed by a clean house that has expensive furnishings and lots of gleaming silver and chandeliers.

"But, he can't have a cleaning service all the time," Peter continued. "Somebody might get suspicious. All of which means that he's the perfect client for a cleaning service that can come and do a deep clean every three or four weeks *between* girls. The maid service comes, vacuums and scrubs, changes the sheets and polishes the silverware. Everything is ready by the time he gets back. And best of all, everything is disinfected and all finger prints have been wiped away."

"Have you seen any evidence of such a service?"

"Yes. An unmarked dark blue van shows up the day after the unusual car is in the driveway. It is there all day. Young women dressed in black—Hispanics—go into the house and come out of it. The van drives away."

"So what's the plan?"

"I want into the house the next time the cleaning service comes."

"By warrant?"

"No. I want one of our people to go to the door under the guise of being a neighbor, and ask questions about the cleaning service."

"What good does that do?"

"Results in a business card, perhaps. But I'm guessing the cleaning service might be an off-payroll, cash-only arrangement. So, our operative will ask to see an example of the work the service performs—check out the bathrooms, bedrooms, and so forth. Eyes wide open during a walk-through. Perhaps lift some prints if the opportunity is there. Operative needs to show up within minutes after the service arrives, and ask for a before and after look. Comes back several hours later for second walk-through."

"And you think maids are going to allow entrance? Wouldn't that be totally against the rules for them?"

"Normally," said Peter. "But maybe not in this case. My guess is that most of these Latinas would love to have a full-time gig in a suburban mansion, more than to do once-a-month deep cleans. If a person shows up at a door looking very wealthy, and holds out the potential for full-time maid work in a very cushy environment with lots of salary and benefits . . . ."

"Hey, I might apply," said Lance.

"Well, you might not apply, but you might open the door a little wider," said Peter.

"Right," said Lance.

"So—we cover the departure, and then tail the guy all the way to his drop-off, and we'd better be fully prepared for his arrival at this end."

"That's why I'm here," said Peter. "Let's get the trap laid."

"Before we do," said Lance, "I'm guessing that you've told Molly more than I want to know you've told her."

"Probably," said Peter, "so don't ask."

"I don't want to see her shipped off into witness protection somewhere," said Lance. "And more importantly, I don't want to see her harmed."

"Neither do I," Peter said "And if she gets shipped off anywhere, you can bet that's where I'm going to relocate."

"You're that serious?"

"Yes," said Peter.

"Geez," said Lance. "We could end up friends-in-law."

"You could do worse," said Peter. He was glad Lance laughed.

27

Edgar Carvill II was more than a little surprised to find Mirabelle Glossman at his doorstep.

"I didn't even need to ply you with another bauble found in my flowerbed," he said when he opened the door.

"I need to move in for a few days," she said.

"Well, come in off the street to tell me why," said Edgar.

"Mind if I get the place cleaned up a bit before you bring your suitcase over?"

"Not at all. I can send my maid over."

"Not necessary. There's a maid service that works for the guy across the street and down a ways. I had one of the girls that works for that service give me her name and number. She said she'd come and work all night if need be."

"You charmer, you."

"No," said Edgar, somewhat pleased at his old friend's thinking a young woman might find him interesting.

"She's probably holding only a green card. So many of them are in that boat these days. But she's very motivated to make money and very willing to work hard to do so. She'd make a good employee for somebody."

"I'll keep that in mind. When do you want to move in?"

"Tomorrow."

"How long will you be staying in my guest room?"

"Who said I was staying in the guest room?"

"Oh," said Edgar a little stunned and not sure what to say next. "What room did you have in mind?"

"Whichever room looks out on the street toward the north."

"That would be *my* room."

"Well then, that's where I'll stay."

"Are you going to tell me what's going on?"

"Of course," Mirabelle laughed. "You're going to be part of it up to your eyeballs and you will never be able to tell anybody about it."

"Is it something illegal?"

"No. Supremely *legal*, actually. But one of those things that if you know too much, you might be taking what you know to your grave."

"Dangerous then."

"Not if you stay quiet."

"Mums the word. It will be nice to have your acerbic, stylish self in residence, Mirabelle."

"Call the maid."

"Yes, Mirabelle."

"And stop calling me Mirabelle. You've always called me Belle. Get back to it."

Edgar Carvill II realized that he was smiling. He hadn't smiled in a long time.

28

"Peter!" Molly said brightly. "You're not going to believe my news."

"Probably not. I'm just calling to tell you two quick things. I'm between meetings, pouring myself a cup of coffee in the apartment kitchen."

"Alright, I'm listening."

"The Christmas Deco Depot caper is big. National and international. You know nothing. Ellen must not be told anything. Have her come to your house, maybe, and walk from there."

"Oh my."

"And number two, don't be surprised if you see Grams in your neighborhood—or at least her car."

"But that's what I was going to tell *you*," Molly said. "I saw her driving away from Mr. Carvill's house yesterday afternoon. She didn't see me. I didn't think much of it . . . but then I saw her driving into Mr. Carvill's open garage *this* afternoon."

"Right. And you don't know anything about it."

"Is it a *secret*?"

"Semi."

"Is it a secret *affair*?"

There was silence on Peter's end. He hadn't thought about *that* potential angle. But it was a possibility . . . and it made for a good excuse not to tell Molly more than she needed to know.

"We need to keep it just that," said Peter.

"My lips are sealed," said Molly.

"How's everything else?" Peter asked.

"Great," said Molly. "Oh . . . I have even bigger news than spotting your Grams in the neighborhood."

"What's that?"

"Mr. Epstein . . . actually, he is Dr. Epstein, a retired botanist and former professor . . . is legal."

"Which means?"

"He has a license for growing hemp—he sells it to legal pharmaceutical processors. Showed me the official document, signed and sealed and very official."

"Best news I've had all day!" said Peter, laughing. He knew he'd need to check out the full story, but it was a welcome relief to think that Dr. Epstein might be totally in the clear.

"I thought you'd be pleased. I was."

"I just hope the document he showed you wasn't some kind of smokescreen," said Peter, putting special emphasis on *smoke*.

"Very punny," said Molly.

"Thank you," said Peter. "You know—Molly Herman—one of the things I love about you most is that you are never *spaced out*—like too high to know the direction of mother earth."

Molly laughed. "Any chance you will be coming home soon?"

"Not right now."

29

On the one hand, Molly was sorry Peter wasn't going to be in town for a while. On the other, she was glad. There were just too many things to do in preparation for Peter's surprise birthday bash—at least the part of his birthday party that *was* surprise and was definitely shaping up to be *bash*.

The invitations had been purchased, addressed, and sent. Grams had been great in her compiling of the list, and had patiently provided explanations about relationships and personalities for each person being invited.

The helium balloons had been ordered. She could only imagine what five hundred brightly colored balloons would look like in clusters of five held together with massive ribbons, equally bright in color.

The work on the large poster-board signs was progressing. She had met with the sign people the day before and was impressed.

"Sale signs?" the project coordinator had asked her when she and Grams first called upon the sign company.

"My idea is to have a range of items—one per poster. We'll put them on easels throughout the party area. Some of them should be inexpensive items, relatively so. Some expensive. The picture of the item should fill the poster board, and then a price sticker should be attached. You can work out how that should be done. It needs to be read easily. And each picture needs to have a number—large and plain and easy to find."

"Is it a game?" the sign people asked.

"Yes," said Grams. "The only game we are going to have. People will have score sheets, and they will have to determine if the price on the items is a current price, or a discounted 'sale' price. And then, they will need to circle the item on their score sheet that they believe has been discounted the *most*."

"Will there be a prize?" asked Molly.

"Two prizes, I think," said Grams. "I saw this done once, but it was a long long l-o-n-g time ago. Let us see, now . . . . One of the prizes will be a chachki of some sort. That will go to the person who has the FEWEST correct answers. We'll state that the item is actually an extremely expensive heirloom from some distant land, and that it would never be put on sale . . . it will be fun. I may have just the item in my garage, come to think."

"And the other prize?"

"One prize will go to the person who has the most correct answers AND has selected the item that is discounted the most."

"And that prize will be?" Molly asked.

"The item pictured on the poster board!" said Grams. "Or maybe something else I can scrounge up."

Grams had put Molly in charge of selecting items, determining false and true prices for them, making the score card, and so forth and so on. It was a fun challenge.

The rest of the plans had been fairly straightforward.

The cake was ordered. Actually, the cake would be presented as tiers and tiers of exotic cupcakes, on a cake-stand that was unlike anything Molly had ever seen. She had counted eight different places where a three-tier platter of cupcakes might be put. *Who knew?* she thought. And then realized that somebody knew, she just hadn't known.

The caterer had been hired.

The menu had been set.

The chachki had been retrieved from Gram's garage.

The band had been hired and the music list presented, discussed, and edited.

The venue was secured, and cleaning and refurbishing were under way—that was Grams responsibility but Molly was pleased that she was in the loop for almost daily updates.

They had agreed just the day before on the poster board items, and the grand prize.

Molly loved spending another person's money—carefully, yet in such large amounts. She loved the entire "arranging" of the event.

She admitted to Tams, "I've never been back stage in the planning of a rich person's party. It's amazing."

"A far cry from a July picnic potluck down on the farm," said Tams.

"Far far f-a-r cry."

"But you sound as if you are having a lot of fun with it," said Tams.

"The best part is getting to know Peter's grandmother better. She's an amazing woman. More wealthy than any person I'll probably ever know. But very down to earth, and mentally, she's as sharp as a tack. She's up on everything. She said it's because she watches the biography, science, and history channels."

"Really! That would do it."

"And . . . that she has watched the same soap opera for twenty years!"

"You're kidding."

The last time we got together—just a couple of days ago, she looked at me and said very dryly, but with a wink, "You know, this is turning out to be almost as complicated as a wedding."

"But it isn't, is it? You aren't telling me, are you Molly Herman that this is a surprise wedding, not just a surprise birthday party?"

"No, no, nothing like that," Molly said. "But there is a little bit of a surprise, Tams."

"What's that?"

"Grams insisted that I invite you and the girls—and Lance, too, if he can come. She said she would pay your way here."

"Wow," said Tams. "Say YES. I'll make it happen—at least for me, probably for the girls. Would they be welcome at the party?"

"Oh, yes, we're having clowns and circus types and other things going on. The waiters are all in costume. There will be a guy making balloon sculptures and another guy doing a little puppet show. It's all on a circus theme."

"Really?"

"Last time I talked with Grams, she was mulling over whether we should have bumper cars of some type transporting people from the parking area to the party venue."

"Amazing . . . . But back to the idea that this was as complicated as planning a wedding. What did you say when she said that?"

"I didn't say anything. I just smiled . . . and I probably blushed. I've got to admit, though—the idea of planning a wedding is not as uncomfortable as it once was."

"I knew it! I knew it! I knew it!" Tams said.

Molly smiled. She felt excitement, too, but felt compelled to say, "I'm not going to let you come to this party, Tams, if you are going to be that wedding focused."

"I promise I'll be good."

"Discreet."

"That, too," said Tams. And then she asked a question that Molly had not considered. "So what's your present for Peter's birthday?"

His present? Everything was being planned down to the "gnat's eyebrow," as Grams had said. But somehow, Molly had not even thought about the *most* important thing related to Peter's surprise birthday bash. *What do I give a man who has everything?* she thought.

"Still waiting on your answer," Tams said, bringing Molly back to the reality of the moment.

"It's a surprise," Molly said. *And how.*

30

"Dad!" Molly said as soon as her father picked up the receiver. "Are you going to be home tomorrow?"

"Sure thing," Abe Herman said. "Why?"

"I'm coming down. I'll be there for breakfast."

"Great! We'll have the bacon fried."

Molly left a little before five o'clock for the three-hour drive, and as promised, was there by breakfast.

"What brings you here?" her father asked as he opened the back screen door.

"Can you stay the night?" her mother called from the kitchen.

"I'm here just for the day. I have a birthday present to pick up . . . from the back pasture fence."

Amused but intrigued, Abe and Clarisse Herman tried to keep a straight face. There was little they could imagine their daughter might be able to pick up from the back pasture.

After a hearty traditional Herman-family breakfast that "provides fuel for twenty hours," in Molly's terms, she and her father donned waders and, after driving to the edge of the ranch, walked through the soft rain-soaked pasture about a hundred feet to one particular fence post. Molly smiled. *It's still there!*

"Dad, I need the top of that fence post," she said. "See the little carving about six inches from the top?"

Abe Herman stooped to peer closer. "M plus P," he read aloud. "Does that mean something?"

"I carved that in the post with the pocket knife you gave me when I was nine and a half years old. There's one on the next post that says 'T plus D.' Tams carved that one."

"Do you want both of the posts?"

"No, just M and P."

"Alright," said Molly's father as he went to his truck to get his chain saw from the metal box in the back of it. "How about twelve inches worth?"

"Sure," said Molly. "I really only need the part with the initials and plus sign."

Within ten minutes the deed was accomplished, the barbed wire had been reattached to the lower but sufficient stub of the post, and they were back in the truck making their way to the Herman kitchen for a third cup of coffee.

Molly's mother took the chunk of wood in her hand and said, "Care to give me a clue?"

"I carved that when I was nine and a half. The P stood for a guy named Peter. He was visiting his grandfather that summer—at the Insmore ranch."

"You called him Petie-Eye, if I remember," said Abe Herman.

"I did," said Molly. "That's the one."

"I never know you and Petie-Eye were an 'item,'" commented Clarisse.

"We weren't. It was purely a young girl's crush on an older guy."

"Well, a girl can dream," said Clarisse.

"And sometimes dreams come true," noted Molly's father.

"I remember those boys. They were brothers, as I recall . . . Peter had a brother, didn't he? . . . named . . . was it Derrick?" said Clarisse Herman,

"And one summer, a cousin came to the ranch, too. A real city slicker."

"Yeah. One of them was called Outsmore, if I recall," said Molly's father.

"Yeah, that was Derrick. Couldn't hit the side of a barn when we were playing softball."

"And I take it you have made contact with someone named Peter, or at least someone with a name that starts with a P?" Clarisse asked.

"Right," said Molly. "I haven't said anything until now because I wasn't at all sure where things were going, but I started seeing that same boy named Peter—the former Petie-Eye—on New Year's Eve. Things are—well, pretty serious. I may be bringing him home for you to meet in a few weeks or so."

"Really?" said Molly's mother. "We'll try to make you proud."

"He already knows you and loves you, Mom," Molly said. "He has already eaten a dozen or so meals or snacks right at this very kitchen table, remember?"

"How did you get in touch after all these years?" Abe Herman asked.

"He was my mailman," said Molly with a sigh. *Mailman and . . . how much could she tell?* Over the next two hours she told as much as she felt was prudent about her growing relationship with Peter, answering as many of their questions as best she could.

"Was this the young man you first told us about last Thanksgiving?" Clarisse asked.

"No," said Molly. "That was another guy. My relationship with him fell through—pretty abruptly, and somewhat painfully. But I'm glad it ended. I wouldn't have hooked up with Peter otherwise."

"You were feeling that pain at Christmas, weren't you?" asked Molly mother.

"I was hoping it hadn't shown," said Molly.

"Mothers know these things," said Clarisse. "And what about Peter's parents? His grandparents we know, but I've never heard any mention of parents. Have you met them?"

"They died in a head-on collision with an 18-wheeler that skid out of control on ice. Peter was sixteen at the time. He moved in with his other grandmother. I think that's part of the reason they are really close."

"You know," said Abe, "I think I remember reading about that—or maybe talking to Ike Ismore about it. Really tragic."

"I'm glad he had them for at least sixteen years of his life," said Clarisse, who was prone to always looking for a silver lining. "They obviously laid a good foundation for a great human being."

"Speaking of that city slicker kid back then," said Abe. "I think he's back. You called him Lyman, as I recall."

"Right," said Molly. "What do you mean, 'he's back'?"

"Well, one of Insmore's grandsons has moved into the ranch house. Old man Insmore moved into town about six months ago to live in an extended-care facility. He has a nice apartment there and plenty of guys to play checkers and chess with, plenty of channels on his TV there to watch every sort of sporting event imaginable. I went to see him about a month ago and he was watching curling. Remember that thing they do with the brooms on ice in the Olympics? Well, a major Canadian match was on the tube and he was glued to it."

"What about the grandson?"

"Insmore told me he needed to have somebody move into the house on the ranch, mostly for security, and he was hoping it would be family of some sort so he could go out and visit from time to time. And then about ten days ago, I saw a U-haul truck pull in and then last week, I saw a couple leave the ranch in a new pick-up. Saw them later in town—I introduced myself to them at Woody's Hardware. And when I did, he said he had met me when he was a kid."

"It was Lyman?"

"Well, that didn't sound like his name—close, but not really."

"Was it Ian?" asked Molly, trying to sound casual.

"Yeah! I think that was it," said Abe. "And the woman with him introduced herself as Sharon."

Sterilyn? On the Insmore farm? It was a picture Molly almost couldn't conjur.

"He said they had moved down to the farm to help out for a while. Wasn't sure how long they'd be there. Maybe forever, maybe a few months. I invited them to stop by sometime for dinner. Maybe when you bring ol' Petie-Eye down for a visit we can have them over for a true family reunion," said Abe.

That would be interesting! Molly could think of all sorts of reasons to postpone that dinner. She also could think of no really good reason why Ian and Sterilyn had moved into the Insmore house and taken up the life of rural ranchers. She mulled it over all the way back to the city that evening.

Peter, of course, had the explanation.

"Well, let's just call it a preemptive witness-protection move," said Peter when Molly asked him during their phone conversation. "After I met with Sterilyn that day at Grams, Grams suggested to Sterilyn and Ian that they might move down to grand-dad's ranch—to help out, and frankly, I think Grams is hoping that Ian might rejoin the rest of us in the real world and take a liking to old-fashioned work. Sterilyn thought it would be a real adventure."

"Why do I hear the theme song from 'Green Acres' running through my head?" asked Molly.

Peter laughed. "Entirely appropriate, I think. It would make a good remake of that old sitcom!"

"Dad thought he recognized 'Lyman,'" said Molly.

"What were you doing down there?" Peter asked. "I hope your folks are both alright."

"Fine. I just hadn't seen them since the holidays and I needed the drive time to think through some things and get a fresh perspective." *It was partly true.*

"Hope that didn't mean any change in perspective about me," Peter said.

"No—new approaches to some things at work. Perspective on you remains the same!"

"Good!" said Peter, "at least I hope it's good."

"All good."

31

"Are you going to be able to come to the party?" Molly asked Ellen on their next walk together.

"I am. Jerod can come, too. Actually, I should phrase that a slightly different way. Jerod is *willing* to come. He's not much of a party person, but this whole shindig is intriguing to him. Pretty heady stuff for us middle-class folk in the 'burbs."

"A bit heady for me, too," admitted Molly. "I don't mind saying that I'm in over my head but I'm enjoying the swim."

Molly went on to tell Ellen, "I got Peter's birthday present on Saturday. I drove down to my folks house to pick it up." She described what she had retrieved from the back pasture, and about how the carved fence post had first come about.

"Somehow, all of this sorta seems like fate— or maybe it's a God thing," Ellen said.

"I believe in God things," Molly said.

"Me, too," said Ellen, who went on to ask, "Have your folks met Peter yet?"

"No, at least not recently. Not since I started seeing him."

"Do you think they know how serious you are about him?"

"I think they do after our visit last Saturday. Mom asked me if I had really spent time getting to know Peter—I told her he had been out of state. I told her that I probably knew him better *because* he has been away than I would have known him if he had been here in town. I added it up, El, and we've talked by phone at least 85 hours in the last ten weeks. That's a lot of talk time."

"You've counted the hours?" Ellen asked, incredulous.

"It's probably a German-ancestry thing," Molly said with a shrug. "All of the Hermans, for as many generations as I know about, have been sticklers for keeping records of all kinds—diaries, journals, family tree information, annotated address books, ledgers, logs. If you can keep track of it, my family has kept track!"

"Seriously."

"Sure. Dad always called it good husbandry. Mom called it household inventory and budgeting. I think we're all a little obsessive-compulsive about keeping track of the details, but there you have it."

"Eighty-five hours is a lot of time," Ellen noted.

"Mom thought so, too. And Dad was *really* impressed. He said, 'Why that's how many hours of talk time I had with your mother during the first three years we were married!' He was joking, but he was also amazed. 'What do you have to talk about all those hours?'"

"Mom told him to mind his own business but I was glad to respond. 'We talk mostly about my neighborhood and my neighbors,' I said. And Ellen, it's true! We do a lot of that. I said, 'Dating your mailman is like dating the local news reporter.' Dad just shrugged. Mom raised her eyebrows in skepticism."

"But you and Peter talk about a lot more than that," Ellen said.

"We do. And I told them that, too. I told them that we talk about likes and dislikes, beliefs, opinions, the news, the overall cultural trends we see in the world, the meaning behind the meaning of the local political activities, the message we heard last Sunday at church, and on and on it goes," Molly said. "I even told them that we have prayed together several times about various things."

"You've never told me about that," Ellen said. "I think that's very cool."

"Do you really?" Molly asked.

"Yes," said Ellen. "In fact, one of the things that let me know Jerod was the guy for me was that we had prayer together one night, about two months after we had been dating."

"Really?"

"Yeah. We had met in church, but you know how that goes. All the guys in the youth group at a church are not necessarily interested in God."

"How right you are."

"But Jerod was different."

"Do you still pray together?" Molly asked. "Sometimes things change after a couple . . . ."

"We do. Every morning, actually, before he heads off to work."

"I'm impressed. Let's talk about that more the next time we walk. I'm thinking that you can probably help me be more at ease around Peter when it comes to talking about the things I really believe at the deepest part of me."

"Sure," said Ellen. Molly was impressed at how relaxed Ellen was about this, and also glad that it had come to the surface in their relationship as friends.

"I bet your parents were glad to know that this is not just a superficial, go-there-see-that-movie-try-that-restaurant sort of relationship," said Ellen, "if you know what I mean."

"I know exactly what you mean," Molly responded. "And so do they. If I am supremely grateful for one thing, it is that Peter is multi-dimensional and he's very communicative."

"*And* he's a good kisser."

"Well, that too," Molly said. She knew she was blushing, but hey, Ellen was her friend.

"You asked about my parents meeting Peter," Molly said after a few moments of silent walking. "That's going to happen at the birthday party."

"Great!" said Ellen. "That means I can meet him, too. At least meet him when he's not wearing his mailman uniform."

"I saw Grams yesterday afternoon. She loved the photos of the posters I showed her. And she told me that she thought I should invite my parents and my sister and her family to come to the party. She volunteered to have them stay at her house. 'I've got that entire west end of the second floor that never gets used,' she said. 'It would give us all a chance to get better acquainted.'"

"Wow," said Ellen. "I'm not sure my parents would be able to handle Mirabelle Glossman."

"Actually, Grams met my parents years ago—on a number of occasions, when she went down to the Insmore spread to be with her grandsons. I don't remember meeting her, but they do. That's the amazing thing," Molly said. "My parents not only can handle somebody like Mrs. Glossman, they don't even think there's anything all that unusual about her. Maybe they will after they stay in her house. It's like a museum of rich-people's furniture and artwork."

"It's going to be an interesting weekend, Miss Molly," said Ellen.

"And the best part is that Peter is going to *be* here for the weekend of his birthday. Nothing had better happen to that plan."

32

"Peter! You are never going to guess . . . I may have a new job—or at least a second stream of income."

"Really?" asked Peter. "I thought you were happy in your job."

"I am, but hey, there's always a new challenge, right?"

"Well, sometimes . . ." Peter replied with hesitation.

"It all has to do with Dr. Epstein."

"Okay . . ."

"I took my very sick and virtually dying orchid over to his house yesterday. He took one look and marched me to the orchid infirmary section of his greenhouse. The entire hedge of hemp is gone by the way. Harvested and out of there."

"Wow . . . that *is* news."

"There's this amazing set of small pipes all around the perimeter of his back yard. I asked about it and he told me that he ran warm water through those pipes to keep the hemp alive during cold weather, freezing temperatures, and all that. Very innovative, I thought. He also said he has warm-water pipes under the greenhouse. Anyway . . ."

"He treated my orchid and then told me he thought I should leave it there in his greenhouse for a week or so, which is what I did. He gave me a new baby orchid that he had propagated and told me jokingly to try to keep it alive. I promised to do my best. But . . . ."

Peter knew that Molly would eventually get to the point. She always did, but sometimes a little later rather than sooner.

"We were walking back through his house when I saw a fairly large dehydrator on his kitchen table. There was a tray next to it of . . . wanna guess?"

"Leaves."

"Right you are, Mr. Peter Lorgham. Leaves. He noticed that I had noticed and said very matter-of-factly, 'Quality control.' So—I'm not sure if that makes him in possession, but there you have it. And then, he asked me if I smoke pot.

"I told him absolutely not . . . never have, never want to. And he said, 'Perfect!' I asked him, 'What does *that* mean?' and he replied, 'That makes you the perfect candidate.'

"'For what?' I asked and he said, 'to have a greenhouse like mine. The powers that be have asked me to expand my operation. They like the quality of the product I give to them. I told them I had maxed out my backyard and they suggested I find a backyard that I could rent, or work with somebody. You might be that somebody!'"

"Molly," Peter started . . . .

"I know, I know. I said to him, 'Dr. Epstein, are you asking me to build a greenhouse in my backyard so I can grow pot and orchids and get rich?' He said, 'I am!'

"And I said, 'But you said the person who did that couldn't be a user, and that would mean no quality control.' And he said, 'Oh . . . oh dear me . . . you think I'm the one testing this for quality control? Oh no. But my daughter-in-law is. There's no assurance the product she gets for medicinal purposes is from my greenhouse. I let her try my product for comparison sake.' And then he said with a very sad voice, 'She's not getting any better.'"

"Sorry to hear that," Peter said, and Molly could tell he was genuinely sad to hear about another person's suffering. "But," Peter went on quickly, "you aren't really considering this, are you?"

"Well, no . . . not fully. I really don't want a greenhouse in my backyard. But I was thinking about that large room with the west windows of your penthouse—very intense sun, I suspect. They have those new turntables for indoor greenhouses . . . ."

"Don't go there!" Peter said. "It might be too tempting. I'm getting bored sitting here in Oregon waiting for something to happen that isn't happening . . . at least, not yet."

It was Peter's second phone call within the hour. An earlier call had come from Grams.

"Dark green Volvo station wagon pulled into the driveway at seven o'clock, actually 7:08. License plates are Washington state. At least I think it's dark green. Hard to tell in the dark. Do you need the license plate info?"

"No. Our guy following the car can get all that info once it's daylight. But are you sure it's a Volvo wagon?"

"Absolutely. And Edgar confirmed it. He used to own one almost identical to it."

"A one-way return of a car to its homeland," said Peter, thinking out loud. "Are you on watch through the night?"

"Glued to the window like a bug on a windshield," said Grams.

He was amused at her metaphor. There was nothing bug-like about Mirabelle Glossman. He couldn't even imagine that she had ever been in a vehicle that had allowed itself to become sullied by flying insects. Edgar Carvil, on the other hand . . . "What about Ed?" asked Peter.

"He thinks this is a huge adventure. We've played more than two dozen hands of Gin Rummy—I'm ahead 15 to 11. We bring each other food on trays and take turns going to the bathroom. And, he has read almost an entire book to me—I told him I couldn't read and watch at the same time, but I could listen and watch, so he's been reading aloud. Something western. And I've done a little work on an old needlepoint project I found stashed in the back of my guest-bedroom closet. We've talked a lot. I've learned a lot about Ed I never knew—even though I've known him since oxygen was invented."

"You are sounding as if it's been a good friendship renewal?" Peter said.

"You could put it that way," said Grams. "I've never known you to go fishing for relationship information, Peter."

"Well, I told Molly not to be surprised if she saw you in the neighborhood. She said she already had seen you—pulling into the Carvill garage. She asked if you were having an affair with ol' man Carvill. I said you were."

"Peter!" exclaimed Grams. "You *didn't*!"

"Sorry. You can tell her that your definition of affair isn't hers or mine."

"I didn't say 'sorry' about the affair part," Grams said. "I can't believe you referred to him as 'ol' man Carvill.'"

"*Really* sorry," said Peter. "Just a saying. No harm meant . . . but then he added, "And what did *you* mean that you weren't sorry about the affair part?"

"I must hang up," said Grams without replying. "I've got some serious surveillance work to do."

"I'll be standing by for your call. Drink a lot of caffeine so you don't miss the departure from the driveway. That is, as they say, the pivotal moment."

Grams second call awoke Peter at 3:30. "He's just loading up the car—suitcases into the back."

"Great. I'll phone the tail."

"Oh—and Peter," Grams hastened to add. "There are three young women getting into the car. All of them have pillows—guess they are planning to go back to sleep."

Peter hung up, called the guy on assignment to tail the Volvo. And then whistled to himself as he hung up and went to the kitchenette of the hotel suite to make coffee. *Three girls. Jackpot.* He sat down to dial Lance. *Ian has been spotted at our new safe house. Sterilyn is going by Sharon.* It was going to be a busy week ahead. *Why had Molly gone to her folk's ranch—really?* But first, there was just time for a shower and shave before he met Lance downstairs for breakfast.

Molly phoned Tams after she got home from church. "I got the perfect present yesterday for Peter," she said with excitement.

"I thought you said it was going to be a surprise," Tams said.

"I didn't want to say anything until I was sure I had the gift in hand," Molly said.

Tams was impressed with the fence post gift, glad that Molly hadn't had the T+D post removed, and gave Molly her flight schedule for the birthday bash weekend.

Things are shaping up, Molly said. She called Grams to see when they could meet during the week to review the party details, but there was no answer. The answering machine message on Gram's cell phone had said simply, "I'm sleeping in today and playing hooky from church. Call me tonight."

33

F.B.I. Agent Martin successfully attached a GPS device under the back bumper of the dark green Volvo when the car stopped for a BBB—breakfast and bathroom break—at a diner about a hundred miles out of town. Photos of the vehicle were taken and sent by phone to Peter and Lance. License plate information was processed. Owner lived outside Seattle. Appeared to be just an innocent guy looking for overland transport of his car. The agent got good photos of all four of the travelers—sure enough, one man, three teenage girls with enough make-up to give them the appearance of young women in their early twenties.

Capture plans were reviewed. The "net" seemed well planned, covering at least ten scenarios.

And then the long wait and careful watch of the GPS signal began.

"Reminds me of a trip across the Atlantic, and the little airplane that moves across the map to show you where you are in the flight," said Lance. "Boring . . . but mesmerizing."

"It's going to be one of those hurry up and wait situations," commented Peter, saying something he knew Lance already knew. "We're going to be scrambling like crazy by this time tomorrow."

He couldn't have been more prophetic.

The split second that the dark green Volvo blew through Winnemucca on Highway 80, apparently heading for Reno, Lance came to full attention. "New trajectory," he announced.

"Not 950-140 to Lakeview?" Peter asked.

"No, straight through on 80, right on the banks of the Humbolt headed for Imlay."

"Reno," said Peter.

"Who do we have in Reno?" asked Lance.

"We?" Peter said.

"Alright, who do *you* have in Reno?"

"We're covered there. Nevada has legal prostitution, you know. But I'm not sure that's where he's ultimately headed. Not much to be gained by turning girls over into something stateside that's legal."

"Where are you guessing, then?" said Lance. "Frisco?"

"My guess," said Peter.

"And you're well-covered in San Francisco?" asked Lance.

"Very well-covered. Oriental connection is strong," said Peter, "but I'm not sure we should rely solely on the GPS tag we have. I'm going to ask that somebody go out and meet the Volvo, sooner rather than later. We need visual surveillance on this."

Lance looked at his map. How far east do you think they could intercept?"

"Stateline, if they hurry," said Peter.

The intercept actually took place at Truckee, just west of Reno across the California line. GPS plus live, streamed video provided good documentation for a four-passenger dark green Volvo. "Let's hope he doesn't stop for the night," said Lance.

"I doubt he will. He would be smarter to try to make a connection under the cloak of darkness. My guess is a drop-off point someplace between Fairfield and Berkeley."

"Assure me once again that you've got this covered," said Lance.

"Top flight. I've already been in touch with the entire lead team. They're excited to be on this score."

"Do you think we should head south?" asked Lance.

"Not tonight. I think you should get some sleep. The car still has to get to Washington. If we're lucky, we might get two drop-offs out of this deal— one in the Bay area, and one in Portland."

"And that translates into some extra R&R at the end of this gig," said Lance. "I'm ready for that."

"Me, too," said Peter. "I've got a birthday extravaganza that I've promised to attend in 10 days."

"A party?"

"Well, they don't know that I know all that I know. I promised to be home for my birthday. The EXTENT of the party is supposed to be a surprise. But hey, I'm F.B.I. Hard to keep a secret from me, you know," said Peter.

"I suppose you even know what your presents are going to be," said Lance.

"No, not entirely . . . but I know what I'm hoping one of them will be."

"Molly?""

"A yes from Molly."

"A yes?" asked Lance. "Ah—you're going to pop the proverbial question."

"Thought I would. I picked up her so-called party favor a couple of days ago while I was out to lunch."

"A ring?"

"Big enough diamond to make her at least *think* about saying yes," said Peter.

"By the way," Lance said. "Tams and the girls . . . and me, too . . . are invited . . . ."

"It's okay," Peter said. "I told you I know there's a MAJOR party being planned."

"But I was just thinking that my being there might have been the only surprise left."

"It might have been," Peter laughed.

"Uh oh," Peter said in unison with Lance. The green Volvo had stopped at a motel just west of Sacramento.

34

Molly hadn't walked with Ellen in several days and she was eager to catch up with her new friend. They had walked at a record pace. "We should always talk so quickly," Ellen had commented. "It makes us walk more quickly."

"The walk and the talk should match up!" Molly said.

They were not at all prepared, however, to see three police cars and two unmarked black vehicles in Ellen's cul-de-sac as they returned to Ellen's home. Ellen had invited Molly for dinner since Jerod was working late. Molly was glad. Without the invitation, she might have missed the drama. On the other hand, Ellen probably would have called.

Ellen approached a man in a dark suit standing next to one of the unmarked vehicles. He had his cell phone in hand but as soon as he laid it on the hood of the car, she said, "Officer, can you tell me what's going on?"

He asked several questions—and once he was satisfied that Ellen was the occupant of the house immediately opposite the Christmas Deco Depot, and that Molly also had been suspicious of the house, he asked them if he could do a more formal interview.

An hour later, Ellen and Molly found themselves staring at their bowls of soup, a bit dazed.

"It all makes sense the more I think about it," said Ellen.

"Yeah. And it was a very clever operation," added Molly.

"Small pieces of art, jewelry, antique items of value . . . forwarded through mail systems to the point of being nearly untraceable, then sold over the internet to people in far-away places with strange-sounding names . . . ." mused Ellen.

"And everybody along the way upping the price just a bit. Puts a whole new spin on e-commerce," said Molly.

"I guess we shouldn't be telling too many people about this," Ellen said.

"Probably *nobody*," said Molly. "Well, we have to clue in Ginny. She is a near neighbor, after all."

"Right," said Ellen. "I wonder what will happen with Mr. Santa in the blonde wig."

"I have a hunch he won't be seen in the neighborhood for a very long time."

When Molly talked with Peter later that night, he wasn't surprised. He had known the warrant had been issued to search the Christmas Deco Depot, along with warrants at ten other locations in seven states. He just hadn't had the time to call Molly to tell her it was likely to be an exciting evening in her neighborhood.

"Are all the bad guys thoroughly captured on this one?" asked Molly. "Or do Ellen and I need to start walking at the mall instead of on our neighborhood streets?"

"I think you're good," said Peter. "This whole ring of people has been amazingly open in their tactics. Hiding in plain sight, so to speak. They didn't think anybody would connect *all* the dots.

And frankly, we might not have if the Peacock hadn't been found in Carvill's flowerbed."

"Is Grams still hooked up with Mr. Carvill?" Molly asked.

"You know, I think she might be," said Peter. "Go figure."

35

Not only was Grams hooked up with Edgar Carvill II but she informed Molly at their next meeting the next afternoon that she and Ed were going to get out of town after the party—maybe travel around Europe a bit.

"Nothing immoral," said Grams. "Separate rooms. We both need a bit of a break. And neither of us has been to Europe in a while."

"Any place in particular?" Molly asked.

"We're thinking the Czech Republic," said Grams.

"Really!"

"We'd like to make sure nothing has changed in Prague since Slovakia went its separate way. Then again, nothing much has changed in central Prague for several hundred years. We just want to make sure it stays that way!"

All plans were set for the party. The event was now just days away and it was time for double-checking all lists, and then triple-checking them.

For his part, Peter was glued to the GPS. The dark green Volvo had left Sacramento about eight in the morning, and after a stop at a Denny's for breakfast, had made its way into the heart of San Francisco. The four entered a legitimate modeling agency there, emerged a half hour later, and from there, the Volvo and a second vehicle—a van that apparently was well stocked with photo gear—had traveled on to Golden Gate Park for what turned out to be a two-hour photo shoot. "Just the right stuff to make all of this seem supremely legitimate," Peter noted.

"This isn't the guy's first time around this block," added Lance.

After the photo shoot, the dark green Volvo had headed across the Golden Gate bridge and up toward Napa. They stopped there at a house that had no commercial listing—a large old Victorian not at all unusual for that part of California. Set in the middle of a vineyard, it had lots of anonymity, and was virtually invisible from the highway.

"They won't spend the entire night," Peter predicted. He was right.

A little before five o'clock in the morning, the Volvo was on the move again, but this time with only two of the three young women. The team based in San Francisco was ready to move in on the Victorian Villa, as it had been dubbed, and do what they could to rescue the girl and arrest all involved in her abduction. They were under strict orders to maintain as much secrecy as possible, and by all means, to keep anybody in the Victorian Villa from making any calls or sounding any alarms.

"I hope the guy they are sending in as a potential 'customer' can pull it off," said Lance.

"If he doesn't, it could get far more complicated," said Peter.

Slowly, but methodically, the Volvo made its way over to the 505 and then north up Highway 5 through Redding, across the Oregon state line to Ashland and then Medford, and then continued on through Grants Pass up toward Eugene.

"Come to Papa," said Lance as the car approached Eugene, and seemed on a direct route to Portland.

"I wouldn't mind living in Grants Pass one day," said Peter. "Ever been there?"

"No. Is it beautiful?"

"Very. Amazingly genteel little city along the Rogue River. Good fishing. Good hiking. Nice blend of nearby farms and city amenities, all just an hour from the Pacific."

"What took you to Grants Pass?"

"A girl named Koko. Met her at college."

"Maybe you can honeymoon there," Lance said.

It was nice to have a slight diversion from time to time from the task at hand, which all seemed to be coming down to a few hours of intense planning.

"Whoa!" said Peter as the car turned east on highway 126. "Where's he going?"

"There isn't much on that stretch of highway," said Lance, studying blow-up maps. "Over the mountain to Sisters, maybe."

"Bend."

"Bend what?" asked Lance.

"Bend, Oregon."

"What's in Bend?"

"A major drop point," said Peter. "Once he headed up 5 it seemed a slam dunk he was going to Portland. There are faster and more direct ways to get to Bend without going through Eugene."

"Maybe he got a call."

Peter quickly made his own calls. The Victorian Villa had been penetrated, arrests made— one hysterical girl, plus two more rather dazed girls "in residence," were put into the hands of juvenile counselors. A sting set up called for more international players to arrive from the City later that night. The net was spread, ready and waiting.

Other calls revealed that it was highly likely the green Volvo was going to be used to transport two girls from Bend up to Portland.

Peter glanced at the calendar on his desk. *He better not take any more detours,* he thought.

"What do we do about Bend?" Lance asked.

"We get our people from Eugene on the road. They'll miss the pick-up, but they should arrive in time to shut down the drop point . . . it used to be a residence just south of town. Actually, it is a rented house in a pretty exclusive resort area tucked into the woods—they call it Sunriver."

Peter made the alert calls and followed up with the agents as they pursued the Volvo that had a significant head-start over the mountains.

When the cell signal disappeared in the mountains just west of Sisters, Peter availed himself of the opportunity to call Grams.

"I was wondering if you were going to call. The cleaning crew came just as you had said it would—not the day of departure, but the day after. I made my first visit after the van pulled out of the driveway. Figured the 'boss lady' for those girls had left the scene. Three Latinas were doing a very good clean-up, if I do say so. They let me in and I watched them at work for a while. I did exactly what you told me about getting prints. Walked out with a couple of drinking glasses and a few pieces of silverware that were obviously used but hadn't been washed.

"Did you go back later?"

"I did. Unfortunately the supervisor had returned. But when I told her that I had already seen the 'before' state of things, she was glad for me to see the 'after' appearance of the house—fully expecting that I would contact her agency for my own house."

"Great job, Grams."

"Now what do I do with these items I basically stole from that house?"

"I don't think the owner or occupant of the house is coming back any time soon. Hang onto them until I get back to town."

"It had better be in time for your birthday," Grams said. "If you aren't here for that, Molly is going to be mighty disappointed."

"Me, too, Grams!" Peter said.

His next call was to Molly.

"Say a little prayer. This is all coming to a head very quickly."

"Not soon enough for me," Molly replied. "Are you alright?"

"I'm fine. It's a precision puzzle."

The green Volvo was only at the Sunriver drop point for a half hour, and then it headed back up through Bend and to Sisters, and in the cloak of darkness, over Santian Pass to a small hotel at Sweet Home."

"Who's on this?" Lance asked when he came back from a quick nap in his own room down the hall.

"Guys from Klamath Falls are headed for Sunriver to shut it down. Guys from Eugene have called for back-up. They're already in Sweet Home. Looks as if they've stopped for the night. The Oregon crew wants to ensure visual verification so they are waiting until dawn to intercept."

At three o'clock they were alerted by ringing phones. "The girls are walking out the door with a couple of new goons who showed up. Doesn't look as if anybody inside the room was expecting this. Everybody pretty much in nightgowns and robes."

"And the driver of the Volvo?"

"Still inside."

"Alive?"

"As far as we can tell?"

"And our guys?" asked Peter.

"Still watching."

"Do you have an ID on the new vehicle?"

"Dark blue van—older, maybe even late 1990s model. Girls were put into the back."

The reconnaissance car followed the van north. About ten miles south of Portland, the van encountered a massive roadblock of police cars and spike sticks. There had been remarkably little resistance in the predawn tour de force.

A second car was sent to intercept the Volvo, which headed out about six o'clock, also in the direction of Portland.

"What do you want to do about the Volvo driver?"

"Follow him and take him in at the first possible point. We don't want him making any phone calls to check on his girls. Try to avoid sirens."

The Volvo driver was arrested during an early-morning stop for gasoline and coffee a short while later, just about the time the van was corralled on the interstate.

By that afternoon, slave traffic sites in Napa, Sunriver, and Portland had all been shut down. And Peter found himself buried in a pile of forms to complete and reports to be filed.

That night he called Molly, so tired he could hardly keep his eyes open. Molly picked up immediately on his exhaustion. "Can you sleep tonight?" she asked.

"Yes. But by this time tomorrow night, I'll be wrapping things up, and then very early on Friday morning, heading home. I'll be there by noon."

"I can hardly wait," Molly said. "What about the girls? Are they safe? Do you know?"

"Yes. It's the best possible situation. All three of the original girls, and the two additional girls picked up in Oregon, are very glad to be where they are right now. At first, they put up all kinds of resistance and arguments. But the more they heard about their abductors, the more they stopped bemoaning the end to their modeling careers. They were concerned, as they should be, about any legal problems they might be facing. Two of the girls don't want to go back home. Two do. One is stone silent, probably in shock. That could all change in the next few days. But my part of all this is essentially over."

"And the house with the gray trim is on the market again, I take it?"

"Eventually. Not any time soon. There will be lots of evidence to be gathered from there, and there may be an operation set up to handle any people who might have been involved with the Recruiter."

Molly replied only, "Hmmm."

"No," said Peter. "Absolutely not! No removal of the brick in the fence.

"I'm very happy to let the professionals do their work," said Molly. "What time does your flight get in?"

"You don't need to pick me up."

"Yes, actually, I do," said Molly.

"Why?" asked Peter.

"I need to feel your arms around me. Sooner, not later."

Peter didn't argue.

36

As much as Peter knew about his "surprise party," he was surprised at what he didn't know.

He didn't know that Molly's parents, and Molly's sister and family, were guests staying at Grams' home. If Molly was okay with that, he was okay.

He didn't know Grams and Carvill were leaving town two days after the party, headed for Prague. Together! He was surprised to hear Edgar Carvill II refer to Grams as "Belle."

He knew the party was set for Saturday night, but he didn't know the party was going to be on Edgar Carvill II's houseboat at Big Rock Lake. Molly said she wanted to take him out to dinner for a pre-birthday time together on Friday evening after he had a chance to shower, shave, and take a nap, and he had agreed, and then had been surprised when they headed out of town.

Molly told him that there was a new spa about thirty miles from town—a spa with a five-star restaurant. Amazing. People have been flocking out there. Organic. Yoga. Little cabins. A chef that has worked in some world-class kitchens. Sorta like the place they had gone months previously, but not entirely.

Seriously? Peter thought. *Maybe . . . but maybe not.* At the last minute, he tossed the ring he had purchased into his pants pocket, just in case the mood and moments were right.

As it turned out, the spa was real. But it was also not their destination. As they drove past the entrance to the spa—very well done in a tasteful yoga-and-organic design and colors—Peter commented, "Wasn't that the place to turn?"

"I'm going through the back gate."

Before there was any opportunity to get to a back gate, or road, or any other form of back entrance, they dead-ended at the lake. There, a speedboat was awaiting them at a small spa-owned dock. And across the lake they sped until they arrived at the very brightly lit and festive houseboat owned by Edgar Carvill II.

The houseboat had been docked securely, and the lawn area between the nearby boat landing and the houseboat had been fully decorated with tents and tables and balloons and all sorts of buffet and beverage stations. Clowns and ballerinas and other fanciful characters were strutting about, holding out trays with glasses and appetizers offered on toothpicks. Children were chasing one another.

And yes, Peter was surprised. After all, it was the day *before* his birthday!

"I take it there's no surprise party at the club tomorrow night," Peter said wryly.

"N-o-o-o," Molly said. "Grams told me that when you were eight you wanted a surprise party and nobody knew it . . . and therefore, you didn't *have* a surprise party. So, she wanted this to be the surprise party you never had, but wanted."

"Aha. I don't recall ever saying that I wanted ballerinas at the party . . . but the clowns are good."

A ballerina brought a tray of appetizers to Peter and Molly about that time, and at the same time, handed them both "bid" sheets.

"What are these for?" Peter asked.

Molly answered. "See the large poster boards scattered around the yard. They have two purposes.

One is to force people to move about, mingle, meet and greet. The other purpose is a real game. Actually, my dear Peter, this is the only game at your party."

"Game?"

"Grams said that when you were a boy you made up a game called Higher or Lower. You'd bring her photos of things from magazines and then make her guess as to whether the price you had tagged on each photo was higher or lower than the actual cost."

"I remember! We'd set a game night and then we *each* showed up with ten photos with price tags on them. The person who had the fewest correct guesses had to buy the other one an ice cream cone—double scoop, and in my case, a cake cone, in Grams' case, a waffle cone."

"Well, this is the same deal. Person with the most correct guesses gets a really nice prize."

"What is it?"

"Can't tell. But it's worth playing the game."

"I always thought that would be a good board game," said Peter. "Only problem was that prices tend to change, and you could never tell if something had gone on deep discount sale to entice buyers in the door."

"Hmmm," said Molly. "Not a bad idea. In this day and age, with electronic access to just about anything, it might be possible to keep those prices up to date. Could be the next Monopoly."

"On the income scale, that might even beat out a greenhouse with hemp."

Molly laughed. And they both made their way to various boards, taking time to greet guests, many of whom Molly had never met before. She loved being introduced as "one of the two most important women in my life." She knew the other woman was Grams so she felt no jealousy, but nonetheless, she was always glad when Peter qualified his response by saying—"Grams and Molly—a guy doesn't need any more women than that."

For her part, she introduced Peter to Ellen's husband by saying, "You may have never met our mailman, Jerod. This is Peter."

"You're our mailman?" Jerod asked, looking to Ellen for reassurance that he hadn't been caught in a terrible faux pas of a joke.

"Well, I *was* your mailman," said Peter. "I got kicked upstairs to do some national planning for the feds." It wasn't a total lie.

"I've never seen such a houseboat," said Ellen. "I can see why Mr. Carvill would rather live here than in our neighborhood."

"Somebody from our neighborhood owns this houseboat?" Jerod asked. "Who knew? I didn't think anybody was anybody in our neighborhood." And then in something of a parody of the old "Cheers" television sitcom opening song, he added, "The ol' neighborhood where nothing ever happens and nobody knows your name." Ellen and Molly exchanged smiles. It was probably best to keep Jerod clueless.

As for the houseboat—Molly hadn't seen it for several weeks and she, too, was amazed. It had been power-washed, repainted, and completely outfitted with new furniture, appliances, and fixtures. The brass shone, the life buoys were all new, and dozens of Chinese lanterns added just the right amount of glow power. A band provided music to span three generations and the guests found it extremely easy to move onto the dance floor almost before they knew there was a dance floor. It had been a recent addition to the lower deck.

Grams sure has been a busy woman, she thought.

Molly was surprised to see Peter so intent on completing his bid card . . . which he did well in advance of the eight o'clock cut-off time She was pleasantly surprised that he *wanted* to dance with her on the houseboat. She was not at all surprised to find that he moved with grace and skill among the various pockets of people—the very polished conversationalist and also an eager listener.

Tams and her family were impressed.

"Haven't I seen this guy somewhere before?" Tams asked.

"Of course. He's Petie-Eye. Have you *forgotten*?" Molly replied.

"No, some time, some place more recent than our childhood," said Tams.

"The well-scrubbed types often look alike."

"Yeah. But he's too many well-scrubbed social cuts above the average postman for me to think he's *only* a postman."

"You don't know enough postal clerks!" Molly said with a laugh. She didn't need to encourage Tams' walk down memory lane. She had managed to greet Lance without giving any sign whatsoever that she knew about his relationship with Peter. That relationship was for Peter and Lance to explain in their own terms and in their own timing. She liked being "in the know," however. And she knew that Lance had not revealed much, if anything, about Peter when Tams said to her in all innocence, "I'm really glad Lance could break away from his assignment in Maine. Just look at him! He's having a great time."

Lance had taken his daughters out onto the dance floor for something of a three-person rumba. They won the laughter and applause of all who stood nearby.

Molly noticed that her parents were among those applauding. She didn't recall the last time she had seen her parents out on a dance floor. In fact, she didn't recall *ever* seeing them dance together.

"You and Dad can dance?" she said to her mother with a dose of surprise in her voice.

"Of course we can dance," Clarisse replied matter-of-factly.

"But where? When?" asked Molly.

"In the living room after you and your sister went to bed," Clarisse said. "All you need is a radio that plays the right songs, and rugs that can be rolled up or pushed to one side of the room."

It was a fun surprise for Molly, nonetheless, to see her father skillfully maneuver her mother around the small dance floor as they held each other cheek-to-cheek.

One of the surprises to Peter . . . and frankly, to Molly and Grams as well . . . was the arrival of Derrick and his wife. Derrick had said they wouldn't be able to make the party that weekend, but he had been able to arrange a substitute for the important meeting he had been summoned to attend. And there he was, little brother with lots of teasing and some great stories to tell about birthday parties in the past. Grams beamed from a distance. She had always been glad for a good relationship between Peter and Derrick, and no more so than now.

Ian and Sterilyn had also sent regrets, but unlike Derrick and Patti, they had not shown up. Molly, Peter, and Grams all knew why. And oddly enough, nobody among the party-goers seemed to notice their absence or ask about them. It was Peter's night from start to finish.

About nine o'clock, just before the guests with children seemed to think the evening was sufficient entertainment for their little ones, Grams called the party to attention and the winner of the poster-bidding game was announced . . . a guy named Merton, who looked every bit the accountant. "He's actually the owner of a department store in a neighboring state," said Peter. "He might have had an unfair advantage."

"I wonder how much he'd take for his bow tie?" Molly asked quietly.

"I'll buy it for you if you want," Peter teased.

"Only if you'll wear it when I want you to wear it," Molly countered.

The prize of the night was a golf cart. Pretty extravagant by all standards. But very much appreciated by Merton. "I'll bet Grams got a great price," Peter said just loud enough for Molly to hear.

"Actually, she got it donated," Molly said. "It's a little older model and Carvill talked the owner of the golf shop into donating it as advertising. See the little license plate on the back—the one with the golf shop's name on it?"

Gift sacks with party favors were handed to the guests by the ballerinas and clowns.

The band struck up a new set of gotta-dance-to-that tunes.

Molly made her way to Grams' car to retrieve her present for Peter. She had arranged with Grams to stash it there, and she was determined to give it to him *at* his party. She set it to one side of the staircase on the houseboat and then led Peter out onto the dance floor for a wonderful medley of three back-to-back slow numbers.

It was about ten o'clock when Peter led Molly off the dance floor and casually undid the latch that had held the velvet rope intended to keep people from climbing the steps to the upper deck of the houseboat. Molly quickly grabbed Peter's gift.

"Should we be doing this?" Molly asked as she quickly moved beyond the rope and up the stairs, with Peter taking time only to relatch the rope before following her, taking two steps at a time.

"I asked Grams what the reason was for the roped off upper deck. She gave me permission to ascend, and even the key."

"Key?"

By this time they were at the top of the stairs, where they found a sturdy child-proof gate that required a key to open it. "Grams and Carvill didn't want any child, or any other person for that matter, to fall overboard from the second deck . . . or to go to the second deck and hole up."

"So why did she give *you* the key?" Molly teased.

"Because I told her I wanted to give you a special party favor of my own," Peter said with a rakish smile and his best attempt at coming up with a lewd look in his eyes. "Besides that, I think she felt she owed me one. She admitted to me in a very quiet tone of voice that I had actually won the prize, but that she just couldn't be regarded as having cheated by presenting me with the grand prize."

"Here," Molly said, thrusting a beautifully wrapped 10-inch long and 4-by-4 square gift into his hands. "Happy Birthday!"

"Wow, it's heavy," Peter said as they made their way to deck chairs by the railing.

"Open it," said Molly.

Peter was puzzled. "I love it," he said . . . "and I'm sure I'll love it even more once I know the full story. The M + P part I get. But shouldn't there be a carved heart somewhere?"

"That would have been too embarrassing," said Molly, as she told him the story about being in the back pasture riding horses with Tams, and about stopping to carve the initials onto a fence post with the new pocket knife her father had given her.

"So, you've been in love with me all this time?" Peter asked, teasingly.

"Probably. But I think back then I would have called it a crush—and definitely a crush from afar. I wouldn't have had a clue how to be a girlfriend to you, or what to do with you as a boyfriend."

"And now?"

"And now . . . it's really easy to love my mailman."

Peter reached into his coat pocket and pulled out a slightly oversized envelope. "Here's what Grams gave me. The two gifts go together, I think."

Molly opened the envelope. It was a ticket of some sort. "Where are you going?" she asked.

"It's an open-ended ticket to a three week cruise on a semi-private yacht in the Mediterranean."

"Oh," Molly said. "When do you leave?" She was having flash images of scantily clad French, Italian, and Greek girls as the deck hands.

"It's for two. Cruise for two," Peter said, aware that Molly had not yet connected the dots—at least not the *correct* dots.

"Oh!" Molly said. "Wow." And then just to make sure she added, "And I get to go?"

"Who else? You're the M and I'm the P on the fence post."

Peter then reached into his other coat pocket and pulled out a small velvet pouch. "And here's your party favor. It sorta goes with both your gift to me and Grams gift to *us*."

Molly gasped.

In all of her trying to imagine a ring on her finger—and especially a ring from Peter—she had never imagined anything quite so beautiful, quite so large, or anything quite so perfectly designed to suite her personality.

"It's the most perfect ring I've ever seen."

"I'm glad you think so," Peter said sincerely. "I'll tell people that you proposed marriage to me in a way I couldn't refuse," he continued, enjoying the dreamy look in Molly's eyes and the uncontrollable smile that spread from her mouth to engulf her entire being. "I'll tell them you hit me over the head with a four by four fence post and said, 'M+P, Peter—don't you *get* it?'"

Molly said softly, "Are you really proposing?"

"I am," said Peter, who fell to one knee beside the deck chair in which Molly was sitting. "Will you marry me, Molly Herman—and go to every New Year's Eve party with me for the next seventy-three years."

"Sure," said Molly as he slipped the ring onto her finger.

Neither one of them could remember how long they kissed, but eventually Peter said softly, "And, oh, by the way, Grams has a big party planned for tomorrow noon at her house. Big lunch for all the out-of-town folks, our closest friends and relatives. She said it could be turned into a wedding if we wanted—she already has a preacher on standby. She pointed out that all the important people are already gathered—my brother, your family, your best friend, and on and on it goes . . . ."

"Or it could just be an engagement party," said Molly.

"Or it could just be an engagement party," Peter echoed.

"Listen," said Peter, calling attention to the music drifting up from the deck below. "They're playing our song."

Sail Away, Sail Away, Sail Away . . . .

What was there to do except smile and resume kissing.

Seventy-three years of New Year's Eve parties—wow, thought Molly.

Why did I only say seventy-three years? thought Peter. *I should have said eighty-seven.*

About the Author

Jan Dargatz is perhaps best known for writing and master editing nonfiction books—personal development, health, Christian living, and Bible study genre. She has written, or contributed writing and editing services to more than 300 works published in the last twenty years. She says about writing adult nonfiction. "These are intended to be light-hearted books, primarily for a woman reader. They are books that are easy to digest on a nonstop flight from New York City to Los Angeles, or as an evening's entertainment by the fireplace on a snowy night. Not everything in life needs to be serious, monumental, or directly applicable to a reader's everyday life. Although . . . there are some fun ideas in this story about Molly and her Postman that could certainly be applied in spectacular ways!"

Other Novellas by Jan Dargatz

The Locals refer to it only as the Incident at the Rubyat . . .

Jillian was tired of Wandering around in Wondering . . .

Meredith arrived at the Party looking tan, rested, and 50 pounds lighter . . .